CORA POTTS

CORA POTTS

WARD GREENE

CUTTING EDGE

ISBN-13: 978-1-957868-58-5

Published by
Cutting Edge Books
PO Box 8212
Calabasas, CA 91372
www.cuttingedgebooks.com

CHAPTER ONE
CATAMOUNT

I N THE EARLY 1900's the Potts family lived at Catamount, which is a flag stop on the Dixie Central Railroad deep in the wiregrass country. Old Bartow Potts ran the general store, one of a clump of shanties perched in a monotony of cotton patches. Over yonder soughed the cool pine woods, and but a mile away Caney Creek kissed the bottoms green. Here, where were only wind and sun and the withered and the bleak, men huddled against a steel link to other men. To the horizon gleamed the rails, and beside them crooked a road that simmered for nine months in the year and in midwinter was a bog.

Twice a day trains broke this desolation. On Sunday there was one. It whipped past the shanties too quickly for the inhabitants of Catamount to catch anything but a jigger of windows. The arms of the signal tower rose gaunt, then dropped with a clank.

Old Bartow Potts—for it was August—spat from his splint-bottomed chair under the gourd vine at the end of the porch. In the dust a hog grunted, and around the corner of the cabin peered a girl.

She was barefoot. As she squatted in the glare of early afternoon where she could see yet not be seen by the figure in the shadow—her chin in her hands and her sunburned legs hunched beneath her—she merged like a wild animal into her background. Her outer garment by chance or many contacts was the colour of the soil; her snarled hair was the colour of the soil; and so were her legs and arms and face. Only the vigilant feline eyes pricked this fusion of tones. She was fourteen and a large girl for her age.

From inside the house droned a voice: "Behold, thou art fair, my love; behold, thou art fair; thou hast doves' eyes within thy locks; thy hair is as a flock of goats, that appear from Mount Gilead. ... Thy lips are like a thread of scarlet, and thy speech is comely; thy temples are like a piece of pomegranate. ..."

Why—wondered Cora—did her Uncle Pledge always read the Song of Solomon? Never a Sunday that he did not settle himself in the kitchen, shake down his galluses, remove his shoes and, sitting with feet cocked in the window against the blessing of a cooling gust, intone verses from the Holy Book. Always the same verses. Uncle Pledge was not an old man. He might better, thought Cora, have spent his Sundays in pastimes of a less scriptural nature. But Uncle Pledge apparently had no hankering for the things of this flesh. He read the Song of Solomon because, he said, it comforted him to consider the marriage of our church and our Lord, and he read aloud because it came easier that way.

Well, Cora was damn sick of Solomon, and of the fields, and her mother's nagging, and her father's strap, though Solomon served a purpose today. Bartow Potts was beginning to wheeze an obligato to the goats of Mount Gilead. In a little while he would be completely anaesthetized. Cora balanced on five toes, extended the others, and examined her leg critically. She was damn sick of bare feet, too. From the cup of her breasts she took a page torn from a mail-order catalogue. The advertisement showed a woman's leg—Cora thought of it as a lady's leg—glorious in silk. For several minutes Cora regarded the advertisement and her own brown calves before she restored the paper to her bosom and crept nearer the corner of the porch. Was the old fool asleep? ... "Thy two breasts are like two young roes that are twins, which feed among the lilies." ... She did not know what a roe was or why it fed among the lilies, but Cora, preening herself, would have faced Solomon with confidence. Had he then called her eyes washed out, her nose snub, her complexion mottled, her figure buxom, the blotches on her arms a stigma of mean blood, he would have amazed and shocked her. She believed at this age, and she mused on little else, that perfection bided for her only beyond the doors of a mail-order house. Remember this, for it is the key to all that followed.

A baby's shrill protest competed with Uncle Pledge, and the figure under the gourd vine stirred. Cora, huddling again, cursed her little brother under her breath. Well, no good trying to slip past that way. She'd risk another. The Potts home and the Potts business were one. A partition divided the shack—merchandise on one side, residence on the other. Entry to the store side by the rear dared Uncle Pledge and her mother, by the front Bartow Potts, who had decreed that to be in the store on Sunday was a sin. When he had napped, he would hobble around the house so as not to jeopardize his eternal salvation. Cora could not wait for that. The store side boasted a window, head high. A push at the sash and the girl, moving dexterously for one so plump, shinned up and over, her burglary invisible to all save God and an acre of sunbaked cotton.

The dim interior, smelling of molasses and tobacco, seemed oddly hostile. She looked around at the flies buzzing above the syrup butts, waited until her eyes grew accustomed to the dusk, drew comfort from the familiar signs advertising nostrums for female weakness. It was a moment's work to find the crocus sack under the scales where her father had stowed it. She snuggled it close to muffle any chink, poked her legs over the sill again, and slid softly to the ground. Running, and looking over her shoulder as she ran, she reached the road and a sheltering curve. There she dropped into a contented strut. The sack rested secure in her catchall with the scrap of paper.

Cora had put several miles of red ruts behind her when she heard horse's hoofs and the jingle of harness. She sat down on a wire-grass hummock until the buggy caught up with her. Its driver was a young man as ruddy as a June apple and dressed by Sabbath dictates in black serge, brown derby and choker collar. His chest was a thunder of pink cravat. Pulling in his nag, he addressed the girl by the wayside.

"Howdy, Miss Cora."

"Howdy, Jim Tuttle."

"Goin' fur?"

"Uh-huh—Caneyville, I reckon."

"So'm I—hop in."

The young man who assisted Cora's progress had known her intimately, as these neighbourly kinships go, since they were toddlers. His father's farm, richer than most, lay but a whoop and a holler—in the local phrase—from Potts's store. Yet, while the buggy spun along through the golden afternoon, he spoke no word to her, but sat bolt upright, breaking the silence only to cluck to his horse or to slap the reins as the animal slowed for an incline or splashed across the pleasant waters of some little stream. As for Cora, she appeared satisfied to gaze mutely at woods and meadows and the breaking cotton bolls without a glance at Jim Tuttle.

Country folk are seldom chatty, but there were added reasons for the silence between these two. On Jim Tuttle's part they consisted chiefly of his clothes, and not so much consciousness that they were new clothes, rather consciousness of the forces that had impelled him to put them on this day. These forces in his mind were vague but none the less effervescent, having much to do with his Sunday freedom and the torpid sunshine and his own glands and the limited social opportunities of Catamount and matters every young man should know. They were the same forces, perhaps, that spurred Uncle Pledge to his favourite scriptures; only, in the case of a less godly individual, they clapped him into fine raiment and sent him jogging to Caneyville where one may eye a gal in the life instead of mirages across the corntops.

Now here was a gal within inches of him, one he had known for years yet never realized before that her body gave off heat and that its brown skin, where it fled into the dress, swelled like a milch cow's udder. The fact put clamps on his tongue and perspiration on his forehead.

Cora, though her bare arms occasionally brushed the person of her companion as she teetered to a thank-you-marm in the road, was not aware either of his blushes or his proximity or for a time, indeed, of his existence. Her own thoughts were not unlustful. They fixed, however, on colder treasures, of which silk stockings were the chief. An image had beckoned her, too, across the corntops, pieced out of mail-order catalogues and glimpses through Pullman windows, and she dreamed on it now in rapture that took no account of palpitating young men in buggies.

The interruption to her reverie a half mile out of Caneyville arrived with something of a jar. It began with the sudden pause of their horse immediately after he had forded one of those babbling streams. "Giddap!" urged Jim Tuttle—and then desisted. Cora became sensible to an increased turbulence of sound. She giggled, and Jim Tuttle turned an even brighter hue. The horse resumed his trot, Cora resumed her fancies, but Jim Tuttle must have figured that two and one, as it were, made something, for they had not proceeded twenty revolutions of the wheels when he swapped the reins to one hand, twisted an arm about Cora's shoulders and squeezed her violently. Whereupon she slapped him with all her strength.

"Don't git smart, Jim Tuttle," said Cora. "I'm a lady."

The bewildered young man settled back into the seat from which Cora's blow had dislodged him, and there-after they rode in dignity unbroken until the buggy reached Caneyville bridge.

"Miss Cora," inquired Jim Tuttle, humbly, "where you want to go to?"

The girl studied the main street of Caneyville, not provocative of excitement on any day and least of all on a Sunday afternoon. For the first time she was shaken in her plans, which, after all, had gone very little farther than simple escape from Catamount. She turned and considered her companion, who blushed under those curious light eyes.

"Where *you* want to go, Jim Tuttle?" compromised Cora.

The late sun found them, with a great many other people, in a tent in a grove on the outskirts of town. After sampling the soda-water of Caneyville, they had been attracted by the sound of distant music and, following the steps of others, they had come upon a medley of wagons and tethered horses and the reason for this jubilee, a sign, "All-Day Preaching." Cora had suggested attendance out of mere curiosity and because she was getting a little bored by her young man. But less than an hour later, a peculiar change, powerful for all that she was scarcely aware of it, sucked at her indifference.

The singing had been protracted and emotional, and now the preacher—a lank, damp prophet with reaper arms and a voice like a witch-doctor's drum—jack-knifed over the pulpit in his final assault on the imaginations of his congregation.

"Oh-h-h-h, brothers! Oh-h-h-h, sisters! I'm sorry for you if you got sin on your soul. I'm weepin' for you if you got sin on your soul! I'm prayin' for you, sinners! For you, blasphemers! For you, adulterers! You strange women and concubines! You liars! You thieves! Ask God to forgive you!—'Save me, Christ, 'fore it's too late! Don't let the Devil and old Death catch me with sin on my soul!'—Git it off, sinners! Wash it off! Wash it in the blood of the Lamb! Sopranners, sing that song! Basses, you sing it, too! 'Washed in the Blood of the Lamb!' "

The tent rocked to a mighty shout, weeping hallelujahs, fervent "Amens!" The preacher shook his arms to heaven, panted over the converts streaming to his feet, shook his arms to heaven again; and the choir sang, some with closed eyes, and the organ bellied and wheezed, and women screeched and men stumbled forward as though drink had their legs—"Washed in the blood of the Lamb! Washed in the blood of the Lamb!"

Cora shrank close to the young man she had slapped. She was hot, breathing rapidly. The crocus sack in her bosom was a hair shirt, pricking and burning as though the loot it hid were the Devil's own nails. Strange things were crawling through her blood on the heels of fear—fear of the wallopings of Pa Potts, of the wallopings of the Lord. She wanted to run one minute and to cry out in ecstatic pain the next. "Washed in the blood of the Lamb! Washed in the blood of the Lamb!" In another instant, she knew, she would fling herself among the mourners jerking in the shavings. Her hand took moist hold of her companion. "Let's get out of here!" gasped Cora.

So they went, their shoulders touching as they strolled, through the grove of pines and past the buggies and the stamping horses, until they came to a dell beside a stream. It was dusk here. The sunset could not stab the mesh of grape-vine overhead. It was cool, too, with an odour of pine and moss and rotting wood. Cora sat down and dipped her hands in the stream and put them to her face. She looked up where Jim Tuttle stood awkwardly on one foot, his forehead a rash of perspiration, and a trembling seized her. She could still hear the singing and the organ's wail, but they seemed far away, shut off by the green wall all around, and closer was the throbbing of her own blood in her ears, and her spittle was thick honey in her mouth.

"Ain't you goin' to sit down, Jim Tuttle?" whispered Cora. ...

So that, stark though the facts are, was how Cora Potts fled from Catamount a thief and lost her virtue in the fleeing. Hours afterward, while a train bore her northward and westward through the night, she pondered these happenings without regret but perplexedly. Why, when Jim Tuttle hugged her in the forenoon, had she repulsed him, yet yielded to Jim Tuttle in the twilight? Religion had done it, she reckoned. Religion was a funny thing. It urged her Uncle Pledge to take off his socks on Sundays and read the Song of Solomon. It had put her, back there in the tent, on the brink of casting herself on the mercy of the Lord, returning to Catamount and giving back the money regardless of wallopings. And it had caused her to make a fool of herself with a fellow she didn't care shucks for. Well, she was good and shut of him, anyhow. She was good and shut of religion, too. She was good and shut of her virtue, for that matter, she reckoned.

She took out the crocus sack and counted the silver and the bills. Thirty-two dollars and forty cents. Plenty for what she wanted, and she'd get work in Peachburg when it ran out. The lamps in the day-coach guttered and stank, doors banged, cinders pelted through the cracks, and a baby cried unceasingly. But Cora rode on velvet, grimy but delicious to her cheek. One dusty leg she studied with half-shut eyes, smiling as she thought how tomorrow's sunup would see her no more among the pickers in the hot, white furrows.

CHAPTER TWO
BEULAH

THE SHANTIES of Catamount were to Caneyville what the town of Beulah was to Peachburg, which was the second metropolis of the state, excelled only by Corinth, the capital. The town of Beulah dozed twenty miles from Peachburg on what one day was to be the Dixie Highway, but which then was only a wagon-track among orchards. Beulah had a bank and a saw-mill and several "stores" and peach-packing plants, and it was a prosperous and serene town, boasting a "rich" man or two and inhabitants who, on the whole, were happy so long as the Lord withheld His hand from blight and frost. God shed his sun on Beulah, and Beulah smiled back at God, and none guessed that calamity could come to Beulah from the direction whence it came.

How Cora Potts, as obscure a baggage as you could find among Peachburg's fifty thousand, could have been calamity's instrument in this matter, is the sort of phenomenon that occasionally makes life seem preposterous. Say, if you wish—as Beulah said—that the Devil conscripts strange tools. The affair remains incredible. One gropes for an explanation—and comes to Banker Tedder.

His name, on the letter-heads of the Beulah Farmers and Traders Bank, was J. Duke Tedder, Vice-President. He was born and raised in the county. Beulah had known him man and boy throughout his forty-five years, and Beulah looked up to him and trusted him. He was superintendent of the Methodist Sunday-school, he had been mayor two terms and might have had a third, he had come practically to run the bank since old Colonel Estes was ailing, and so, though not one of those few "rich" men, in Beulah he was the symbol of money and hence commanded the reverence that all men pay to money. Duke Tedder, of course, was married. His wife had been Jenny Smith, the local school-marm, and she was no longer young when Duke brought her home to the cottage beyond Jester's pond. But she bore him three children and was all that a Beulah wife should be, which is to say that she devoted her life to her family, her home and her religion, and bought a new hat once a year. What she called "hot flushes" began to distress her when Duke was thirty-eight; and thereafter, to inquiries about her health, she was never more than "tolerable."

These, then, were the simple ingredients, manifest to all, in the outward picture of an upright man. It was the only picture Beulah saw; it was the picture Duke Tedder himself would have certified as correct. If, in the substrata of the upright man, impish little bacteria unrelated to their sterling fellows napped and quarrelled and skipped about, how was Beulah to know or Duke himself to suspect? When he had dreams no Sunday-school superintendent could tell at the breakfast table, he put them down to pie and the machinations of Satan.

Consider him, on the September morning he caught "the Bell" for Peachburg on banking affairs bound, and you will see him as he could not see himself. Duke, cross because the Tedder household was in a ferment over washday; Duke, adjusting the bicycle girl calendar over his desk, thinking it pretty, restless he knows not why; Duke, talking crops with the station agent while one eye trailed the progress of Miss Nettie Fly along the street; Duke, fuming on the train steps when he suddenly remembered he must buy that pattern for Mrs. Tedder, and Duke in the smoking-car, silent but tilting an ear toward the two guffawing strangers—this was not alone the country banker, the mirror of decorum, but the eternal goatfoot sniffing Calypso beyond the hedges.

Yesterday, to the forum at Wendell's store, Duke had delivered his opinion, and it was not minced, of him who would set foot inside the Peachburg Casino. Yet, as the hours advanced and delays in business gave him the afternoon unoccupied, the matinee found Duke twiddling before an arcade flanked by billboards, on them gaudy pictures, one of these a lady most prodigal of ankle and flashing her eyes beneath enticing letters, "The Girl in the Sheath Gown." For a while Duke teetered, his hands in his pockets, and then, with a glance over his shoulder, casually mingled with the entering throng.

In Beulah the sun smiled on home and orchard and women flicking soapsuds from red hands; but the Casino Theatre was miles away, a cavern where perfumes rose out of the dark. ...

When the whistle blew at the Acme Mills, Cora Potts trooped downstairs with the women and girls who, like herself, wrung four dollars a week from the racing spindles. Paid, she hurried out alone and walked fast along the street, quite as though there waited for her, too, a home in thrall to bad air and squalling babies and a man's fist greedy for the envelope she carried, or even a boy loitering on the corner to go with her through the twilight. None of these waited for Cora. In Bucktown, that quarter of the city given over to the poor whites, she had a bed and a chair and a wash-basin in a room like a kennel. There she slept, ate and served her gods. They were: (a) a warped mirror; (b) certain articles of adornment; (c) several tattered magazines which she never tired of thumbing. She spelled out the strange, intoxicating words beneath the haughty ladies—brocade, sable, chemise, ruching, suede, amethyst, carmine—and though materials, hues and styles flashed criss-cross in her head, the words were a pageant, and banners waved and trumpets called. Once a week Mrs. Salter waylaid her for the rent and for a few minutes whined her troubles. That was Cora's only companionship. She wanted no other. She had never been so happy.

Pay-day marked the one variation in her delightful monotony. Cora steered a course that brought her shortly to a thoroughfare brighter than its fellows yet raffish to an even greater degree. Black folk and white swarmed here, golden balls glinted in trios everywhere, and in addition to shops, pool-rooms and saloons, the street was peppered with flimsy stands, where, for a nickel, one might fire ten times at moving metal ducks, or "hit the coon and get a cigar," or toss wooden rings at knives and canes and umbrellas, to some of which were attached revolvers and watches. Before such a booth Cora stopped and, paying her fee, let drive at a cleaver in the front row.

The knife which was the object of Cora's enterprise was more appropriate for a bush-ranger than for the ensemble of a young lady of fashion. Dangling from it, however, was a prize less menacing, a pillow of that sort dignified by the adjective "sofa." Its surface was of leather on which was stamped in brilliant colours the vision of a girl in a swing, her petticoats foaming. A young man reclined beneath the swing in an attitude that would have been construed as adoration but for one eye closed in a roguish wink, and roguishness was further emphasized by letters zig-zagging out of his mouth: "O You Kid!" The pillow was Cora's apple of desire. She had come upon it last pay-day, expended fifteen cents in vain casts, and retreated only to yearn more than ever for this bit of fluff which, with its pert legend, seemed to her the essence of modishness and which, furthermore, might be acquired, if one were lucky, by a mere flip of the hand. The something-for-nothing lure already had spread its charms for her in Catamount. She returned to the gallery another evening, when, at the cost of five cents, she smuggled away one of the little rings. With this she practised in her room, a clothes-pin for a target, and attained such skill that anticipation bubbled hot.

But now, though the knife was no further from her than the clothes-pin had been, though she was achieving precisely the same trajectory that had noosed the pin time and again, her rings bounded wantonly off the hilt. When she had squandered an entire quarter, her chagrin verged on despair.

The barker was sympathetic but practical.

" 'Nother jit's worth, lady? If at first—The cane you ring is the cane you win, gents! *and* the knife, the piller and the blue-steel ottomatic six-shooter! Well, the little boy gets it!"

Enviously Cora watched the knife next hers presented to a grinning coloured man. It was not nearly so handsome a weapon, nor did it carry rewards plus, yet here was proof that the trick could be done. She bit a dime indecisively.

Someone coughed at her elbow.

"Want to try again, sis?"

Cora appraised the masher. He was a fat little man in baggy white linen and old enough, she thought, to be her grandfather. She noted that he breathed rapidly, while red mottles came and went in his cheeks, a condition she put down to drink. But one hand, agitating his pocket, produced a jingle which assured her of his good faith.

"Sure, pop!" agreed Cora.

The masher bought her twenty rings. She missed as many times and could have wrecked the stand in her vexation.

"Never mind, sis," counselled the beneficent stranger. Standing beside her, he had offered no advice while she pitched, but continued to breathe heavily. Now he licked his lips. "You're stuck on that p'tic'lar knife, ain't you? Or is it the pillow? Hey, feller, how much is the pillow?"

The barker slewed hard eyes. "Can't sell 'em separate. Ten dollars for both."

White linens crumpled, but spirit was game. "Here y'ah."

Cora, apple of desire under arm and bush-whacker in hand, walked away in a sort of groggy heaven. She had seen more than two weeks' wages flicked over as so much trash, and the spectacle dazzled her more than pride of her new possessions did. Something for nothing? Why, good God, this was fabulous munificence for—hell, she hadn't even smiled! Were men like this—usual? A blinding prospect opened.

"Where do you live, sis?" asked her companion.

She sensed the fingers fumbling for her arm and thoughtfully she transferred "O You Kid" to the other side.

"Just a little piece," said Cora—and cut a smirk his way. "Gonna see me home?"

He saw her home. In the dark outside Mrs. Salter's, Cora waited, but to her surprise nothing happened. Mr. Smith—she had learned that his name was Smith, "Just call me Jack," he said, and he had made an "appointment" with her for Saturday night—Mr. Smith merely shook hands, hesitated, sparred in a patty way at her back, and skipped off. She strolled in considerably puzzled.

As for Duke Tedder, secure once more in the smoker, he allowed himself the relief of a chuckle. By jingoes, if anyone had seen him! But there—he was safe as the Bank of England, nobody from Beulah ever got into that part of Peachburg. He was amazed at how he got there himself. That dang show did it, of course—that and the queer, excited, don't-want-to-go-home feeling nagging him afterward, and then the girl shoving up in the crowd at the cane booth so that their arms rubbed together. He bit a cigar. She wasn't much of a looker, was she? But he'd bet—he'd bet—well, why not say it? He'd bet she'd give a fellow a good time! He didn't begrudge the ten dollars, either. He could have kissed her there on the corner. Sure, he'd seen that. But no use taking chances. The first time, especially. And she with that dang knife. Well, Saturday night—he puffed hard, the mottles came and went in his cheeks, red and saffron, red and saffron, like red thoughts plunging.

Cora arranged the pillow in saucy grandeur on the bed. She stood off, admiring, and her sole regret was that she had sacrificed forty-five cents of her own money before Fate's messenger arrived. And he hadn't even tried to kiss her! She pondered this. Slowly there took form a thought: kisses, like sofa pillows, may seem most desirable when they are most elusive. Had Tedder but known it, his fell mistake was made, not at the theatre or the cane booth, but on the corner, in the dark.

"The fust time I seen him," testified Mrs. Salter at Duke Tedder's trial, "hit was a Sunday afternoon. He come drivin' his rig up to the front door, and Cora she come runnin' downstairs and she says to me, 'Hit's my Uncle Jack from Cattymount.' Fust time I ever heard tell about her Uncle Jack, though I knowed she had a Uncle Pledge because she used to carry on about what a good man he was. Seemed like her Uncle Pledge was always readin' the Bi—"

"Never mind about that, Mrs. Salter," interrupted the prosecuting attorney. "Will you tell us how many times you saw Uncle Jack?"

"Well, not more'n two or three altogether, I reckon. Mine's a respectable house, if I do say it. Gentlemen ain't allowed in the rooms, so Cora and her Uncle Jack most generally went out buggy ridin'. But he'd set in the parlour sometimes, waitin' for her, and I'd talk to him just to be friendly like. I says to him, 'Mr. Smith, it's mighty nice of you to bring yore niece all them nice presents,'

I says, 'and I'm shore she appreciates 'em, but Mr. Smith, do you think it's jest right for a young girl to go dabbin' all them colours and all that cologney on herself? It ain't none of my business, Mr. Smith, but if her maw knew—' "

"You spoke of presents, Mrs. Salter. What were they?"

"Well, fust they was that scan'lous pillow. But lawzy! that ain't a smell 'longside of what he give her after that. Dresses and silk stockin's and cologney and all kinder dewdads, and once I went in to ask her when she was leavin'—she says her Uncle Jack was studyin' about buyin' a house—and she had a pile of money bigger'n a show-dog could jump over. I says to her, 'Yore Uncle Jack's powerful good to you, Cora,' and she says to me, 'He's a good man, Miz Salter!' "

Whereat Mrs. Salter sniffed, as much as to indicate what the future revealed to her about Uncle Jack—and what she suspected then, too!

But, since Mrs. Salter gave her testimony many months after her brief acquaintance with Duke Tedder, and since, with Cora quitting Bucktown as Mrs. Salter expected, the landlady did not follow the girl upward and onward, let us turn to those more nearly concerned.

There was, for example, Mrs. Tedder. Of actual developments she knew the least until all the world knew, yet she must have been first in Beulah to sense, in silent impotence, the onrush of invisible perils. On the morning the Sheriff and old Colonel Estes, shaking like a rickety cart, knocked on the door and asked for her husband, she spoke no word. And throughout the monstrous day, after Duke shuffled away with the men, after her brothers came and told her about the shortage and that Duke was charged with embezzling one hundred thousand dollars— incredible sum!—after the neighbours trooped in with clucks of sympathy and certain of the more motherly whispered rumours of a woman in Peachburg, Mrs. Tedder only shook her head and moaned. She sat behind drawn blinds with her lips shut tight and the cords in her neck like hemp, and, while she tried to think of Duke and the children and herself, she could think only of the woman. Before, when she had thought of the woman, clutching her breasts as the lean flesh shuddered in the glass, she had not been sure. There might have been no woman, no lies, no hidden sins, only baseless suspicions and silly fears. But, almost with the Sheriff's knock, she knew her reprieve of doubt was over. The woman's wraith glided in beside Colonel Estes and, when the neighbours stooped and whispered, the woman stooped, too, in all her hideous beauty, and with her scented hands ripped through Mrs. Tedder's twittering, wizened, old, little heart. Even then Mrs. Tedder was mute.

The rest of Beulah talked of little else. The woman, said the Peachburg papers, lived on the Habersham Road far on the other side of the city. She lived in one of those new-fangled "bungalows," and it was believed, though the house was in her name, that Duke Tedder's money—which was to say, Beulah money—had bought it. As Mrs. Smith she had lived there for nearly a year, and the sumptuousness of her living you would not have believed, only it was right there in print. For reporters had gone to the house with officers of the law, the woman had been arrested as a material witness, her premises ransacked and her entire property impounded, her goings-on investigated, and Duke Tedder's secret was every man's.

Thus you might have read if you chose—and who did not?— the auditor's inventory: rugs, lamps, furniture, music-box, piano, bay mare, surrey, wines, whiskies, rose satin evening gown, broadcloth suits, seal muff, silk nightgowns, silk underwear, diamond pendant, gold and onyx watch, and the list was but begun. Or you might have listened hours on end, in such buzzpots as

Wendell's store, to the tales the newspapers hinted of immoral revelry; you might have chuckled, were you so fortunate as not to be counted among the depositors of the Beulah Farmers and Traders Bank, at the waggeries about Duke Tedder's undreamed talents and the charms of his light of love.

If, however, you were one of the housewives of Beulah, you devoured inventories and gossip with eyes that crackled and ears that scorched and with a strangling in your throat. For that bungalow, those gowns and jewels, the wine and saturnalia, flowed from the savings drudged by knotted hands out of tub and needle and cook-stove, gouged literally from their own flesh, hoarded in the bank they believed safe as the rock of ages—that a harlot might sprawl in Sodom. They hated her, they envied her, and they conjured up visions of a woman lovely as a nereid and wicked as a hell-hag.

Out of all this moonshine one thing was clear: the world had not gone hard with Cora Potts after the evening Fate's messenger arrived. Not ten months separated the acquisition of "O You Kid" from the auditor's report, yet in that time, if half the tales were true, Cora had been as busy as Ali Baba's forty thieves. Admitting exaggerations—each gew-gaw become a Koh-i-noor, every rag a queen's robe—the fact was unassailable that a cotton mill girl from Bucktown had tapped a gentleman for a hundred thousand dollars as surely as once she tapped him for the price of a pillow and a bowie knife. How she did it and her own emotions during the tapping, provided endless talk in Beulah. But, knowing what one does of Tedder's behaviour at that first meeting and of Cora's scrubby dreams then, one may venture a shrewder guess than all Beulah's lurid stories. ...

Was she so fiendishly clever? Picture her on one of those nights when nereid and hell-hag were at their best and worst. She had moved not long since into the little house which Tedder, wavering between so large a sum of money and fear of discovery, decided upon after his panics in cheaper but riskier quarters. The purchase must have been his own idea. One may even conceive the hocus-pocus over the note as so much mud to her, dictated again by Tedder's caution. (At the trial Cora's seeming ignorance of Tedder's affairs exasperated the prosecutor to rhetoric, but when he termed her a Jezebel, there is reason to believe he complimented her.)

Picture Cora returned from an afternoon's shopping. The mare is stabled, the parcels dumped on the bed; from the kitchen float rich savours and a husky contralto; Cora, a nip of whisky before her on the dresser, approaches the rites of toilette that she may please her expected lord. But first, for the house is still a novelty, she must dawdle about, smoothing the plush and golden oak, putting a cylinder on the graphophone, switching electric lights on and off, pausing in the bathroom to twiddle and pull out of sheer delight in the plumbing, so different from Catamount. She rips open the parcels. On the counterpane grows a heap, from licorice "nigger babies" to vermilion ostrich plumes. Cora adores and regrets at the same time. Somehow, though God knows she spares no expense, nothing she buys ever looks right for long. Today she spent—she doesn't know exactly what, but damn near all the money Jack gave her day before yesterday. Well, no matter—to quote Jack, there was always more where that came from, out of his mysterious "business." Cora rakes the heap to one side, sits down and pulls off her stockings. She sighs. It costs a mint of money to be a lady, doesn't it? And hellish trouble bathing all the time! A "nigger baby" tempts her. She sucks it meditatively, wonders what became of that yellow dress, takes another sip of whisky, and decides to forgo the bath. After all, there's nothing like a little sensen to make a girl smell good. ... At nine, Tedder. ... If the night is balmy, they sit on the veranda. Thence, through the house, a murmur and now and then an intelligible word drift back to the kitchen, where black woman and black man smother their laughter with the delight of children spying on their elders. "Heah what she say?—'Gimme, gimme'—onliest tune she sing—'gimme, gimme, gimme!' " From the front, hushed for a while, stir other sounds—a creaking and a scuffling and a voice sharp in reprimand; gruff apology; the murmur once more. Black man doubles in silent glee. "Lawzee, white man git him a li'l lovin'?—Lawzee, ef I'se dat white man—! You heah me, gal? Ef I'se he—!" The murmur in front goes on. And perhaps it will not be interrupted again, but will rise and fall, decorous as prayer, long after the kitchen lights are out and black laughter melts beneath the stars. ...

Cora was trying out a new face lotion on the night they arrested her. She was forever having torments over her complexion, which retained the stain of country wind and sun against all the patented assaults she made upon it. When that cornfed look persisted, she would drown her sorrows in more cologne and bolster her vanity by loading her person with ornaments. Of these she possessed a great variety—rings, pins, bracelets, necklaces—most of them cheap but flamboyant pieces which she kept in a shoebox and never tired of "trying on," like a child fussing with paper dolls. She was eyeing the effect of abalone ear-rings framing her pudgy and still greasy cheeks when the sheriff thundered at the door and she was dragged off to Peachburg police headquarters with scarcely time to wipe her face or put on her clothes.

When Lawyer Phil Bruce, hungry for any pickings, was admitted to her cell, he found her a picture of despair. Cora sat on the edge of her bunk in a rose and gold evening dress. Fat hands blazed with rings, beads jangled like a harness, hair straggled across her eyes, one shoulder-strap had popped, and her flesh humped out blotched and dirty. Only an hour had passed since she watched the deputies rummaging through her treasures, and the tears she had shed then were dried in powdery blobs.

"What a moll!" thought Bruce, who had looked for a houri.

He told himself he knew the line to take.

"Have a cigarette, kid."

Cora glared moistily.

"Ladies don't smoke, you damn fool!" she sobbed.

Later, when Bruce and the turnkey roared in the corridor, she wondered what was the joke. And when Bruce, securing her release on bail, proposed to take his fee in other coin than money, she told him she was not for sale.

"Go on!" scoffed Bruce, inflamed by Cora's cologne. "Didn't Tedder buy you?—And a heluva price he paid!"

"He did not," denied Cora. "We was friends."

Bruce roared again. Yet, when Tedder's trial came on, he was witness to an incident that confounded not only him but all Beulah.

The day was outstanding, for it marked Cora's sole appearance on the stand. By her attorney's advice, she had "laid low" in a cheap Peachburg hotel while lawyers fought over the bank's wreckage. Meantime Beulah had yearned for a sight of "Tedder's woman," for whom he rotted in jail and she not making a move to see him or even write him a letter. Now the State had called her, ostensibly to drive home the last nail in the defendant's guilt but actually to grind out of the witness, if possible, the secret of various missing assets which escaped the auditors in the mess wrought by Tedder's jugglery. Earthquakes could not have kept the wives of Beulah from court that day, for she must materialize in the flesh—the strange woman of the Bible, the Delilah, the whore of Babylon.

The witness sat with her counsel, who, to do him justice, had protected ably her interests in disputed properties. While Bruce whispered encouragement during the preliminaries, Cora did not stir, though she must have felt like a fly under the microscope. Judge and jury were gawking. Lawyers tilted their chairs for better views. Of the folk squeezed in doors and windows, none but sweated there to see the siren. And she, sitting so placidly, never lifting a finger save to smooth down the dress about her fat calves, never glancing once at the little man who shambled in with a bailiff and took his place but a table's length away, she for all her plumes and velvet, was palpably no siren; only a girl with thick ankles and a moon face. Beulah gaped at this pudgy Ruth for whom the gleaning had gone so well, and Beulah looked at Boaz and could not understand. Nor did what followed enlighten them.

The prosecutor, hacking away on the trail of lost funds, had carried her again and again over the details of her life with Tedder. Cora remained unruffled. She had never heard of stocks, bonds, notes. Mr. Smith—she spoke the name naturally—didn't talk business. She had thought—she couldn't say why—he was in hardware. Yes, he gave her money. How much money? Honest, she hadn't a notion. Mr. Smith was educating her. He was her uncle—well, a cousin, anyway—she never could keep track of relatives. Mr. Smith had said he wanted to adopt her. He was always the perfect gentleman. And she, of course, was a lady.

"Do you mean to tell this court you and Duke Tedder didn't—?"

In his indignation the prosecutor bawled a homely phrase which the judge, in the interest of clarity, let pass. The phrase had the merit of being understood by the witness.

"I should say we didn't!" retorted Cora, with asperity. "He never even asked me to!"

Beulah guffawed. The judge rapped for order. The prosecutor glared. "Your honour, it is my conviction that this witness is lying. I demand—"

"Ask him!"

Cora's interruption came without heat, yet so positively that even the prosecutor followed her pointing finger.

The prisoner sat a few feet below her in the same trance he had maintained since he offered submissive wrists to his captors. Of all those at his trial, he had seemed the most remote from what was going on. His white linens hung dirty and wrinkled. In the last few weeks he had become thin. The dumpy, bald little man was now a dumpy, bald little ghost. In the way he crouched, without ever taking his eyes from the floor or his hands from between his knees, there was the suggestion that he might wilt suddenly into a little heap of dust in a soiled, white bag. He had not looked up during Cora's testimony. But, with the hush, he roused from his contemplation of pine boards and his eyes scuttled to hers like dead leaves harried by the wind. His mouth opened and shut without a word. There was no sound anywhere for a moment—then, far back in the courtroom, a choking noise. Only her nearest neighbours knew that this was the prisoner's wife.

"Come down, Miss Potts," said the prosecutor.

And that was that. The authorities never unearthed those missing funds, though Cora lost nearly all her pretties.

Tedder got fifteen years. In State's prison, a few months later, he died. When, toward the end, Mrs. Tedder would come to see him, he did not know her, but mooned about his cell, kissing and crooning over a lock of hair that had come to him in the mail. The hair was Mrs. Tedder's. She could ill spare it, but, as she frequently told her sisters in the church, she was a Christian woman and there was little enough she could do for Duke. …

At the New York Hotel in Peachburg, where guests could never trust the linen but might be sure of other comforts, Phil Bruce waited to collect his fee. The large, soiled man, wedged into a rocker in Cora's murky chamber, appeared as clumsy as he felt. The business, for all the publicity he had procured, hadn't moved to his perfect satisfaction. For one thing, due to Cora's stupidity or reticence—he wasn't sure which—he hadn't the faintest notion whether the bill in his pocket would be received with a shriek or a nonchalance that would make him swear for not doubling it. A heluva note, for a lawyer's client to hold out on him both her confidence and her favours. Not so much as a kiss or a hug had she given him, and Bruce, pulled between the itch to ravish her pocketbook and the thought that, if he went easy in one direction, he might triumph in another, had been in a sweat for the last hour. Waiting for Cora to emerge from the bathroom, he was acutely conscious both of the four figures he had written and of the intoxicating odours around him. Dammit, there was something about the ungrateful hussy, blowsy though she was, that got his goat! Was it just possible she had told the truth that day on the stand?

A lock clicked. Cora came out loosely wrapped in pink and green.

"Hello," she said. "How's tricks?"

Bruce steeled himself against the miasma of fragrance, fumbled for the envelope, thrust it toward her and resumed his seat with temples damp. The devil! He wished she'd stop switching herself around.

"A heap of money!" remarked Cora.

"You said—"

"I know ... Hard cash ... You was willing to take it out another way, wasn't you?"

What in thunder was she driving at? He was taken aback for an answer, for she stared at him as though he were so much furniture. Had he not been flustered, he must have read her mind easily. Not, perhaps, in all its windings from Catamount to swift luxury to sudden deprivation; not in its grasp of the fact that affluence can be acquired with a wink yet lost overnight. He did not know that Cora was watching bank-notes, newly precious, winging away from her just as clothes and jewels had winged away from her—and all for a little squeamishness over an operation which, in her time, she'd experienced when a few hymns instead of grave economic reasons were the urge. Bruce might have seen the calculations in her eyes as plainly as though they were written on a blackboard, but he sensed only that she, too, was breathing quickly.

"Do you still want to trade that way?" asked Cora.

She flicked her lashes and though she was sitting across the room, which had no light save a lamp beside the bed, Bruce imagined he felt the flame in her eyes.

The lawyer nodded, cursing himself for a fool.

She walked over, the bill outstretched. The barrage of cologne undulated before her.

"Mark it paid, will you?"

Not until he had signed and Cora had locked the receipt in her trunk did she disrobe.

She was, if you like, mercenary, heartless, wanton. But neither then nor later did she find that these three qualities were obstructions in the road she climbed toward her star.

CHAPTER THREE
PEACHBURG

"WHY," SAID the woman in Room 42, who suspected Cora of having salted thousands, "why don't you get in some payin' business, dearie? I got a gentleman friend that I'll give you an interduction to him—"

Cora received as a voyager receives all seasick remedies, never knowing what may prove efficacious when the boat rocks, a paean on the gentleman friend and the letter to him. But she froze at Room 42's whine for a loan.

"I'm just as broke as you are, hon," she said. No use letting everybody know your business. ...

That had been before Tedder's trial, while the threat of State's prison still menaced the State's star witness along with Tedder. After the Sheriff led the little man out for the last time and the witness turned her back on Beulah, after she vanished into her Peachburg incognito and wound up such loose threads as her lawyer's bill, she took out Room 42's letter and examined its address. Here was chance in an uncertain future:

Major Archibald Waveroon
Ajax Building
Introducing Miss LaMont

The name of Thelma LaMont had enchanted Cora in a novel by Bertha M. Clay, the first and the only book she had read up to this time. When Bruce advised a pseudonym, she chose Thelma LaMont instantly. As Thelma LaMont she was known at the New York Hotel, as Thelma LaMont she went where Cora Potts, of Beulah notoriety, would have been ejected, and as Thelma LaMont she had to her credit in the Second National Bank of Peachburg the sum of five thousand dollars, overlooked by the auditors, since even auditors do not rifle the pages of old magazines. Snuggled among the pretty ladies and the luscious words, Cora had hoarded those fifties and hundreds released by Tedder as his moral fibre collapsed and Cora's sense of thrift harkened to the gong of Fate ahead. The sum, save for a few furbelows the law had spared her, represented all the buried treasure from her buccaneering.

What should she do with this money? Live on it until it was all gone? Then back to the cotton mill? Memory of the spindles scorched her like the breath of an ogre. She had come a long way from Bucktown, and it would be a longer, harder way back. No, she must get something else to do—"some payin' business." And you never know your luck. This Major was a big business man, 42 had said, a gentleman, an old gentleman, but you know what them old men are, dearie. No harm trying, anyway; vaguely the already forgotten ghost of Tedder, himself no young man, spurred her on. ...

Behold, then on a fair October morning, Cora at her mirror, preparing herself for sortie. While she stroked and daubed, her musings were practical. The past, Tedder, the law, Bruce, along with religion and virtue and Catamount, she was good and shut of. The future flashed bright prospects, but the way was dim. Her concern was the present. And the present was the reflection she beamed and scowled upon.

Nothing—so Cora's thoughts ran—makes or breaks a lady like her teeth. Eyes, nose, mouth count, but they are as God gave them to you; if they offend, you make the best of them, for you can't pluck them out whatever the Bible says. Hair you can do something with—she considered the dun hank in her hand—dye it, for example. How would she look as a raven brunette? But hair, after all, is subject to the hat at the crisis of first impression, such as meeting one's Major Waveroons. The figure tells, of course. Cora stood up, and the green and pink dressing gown whisked away from her buttocks. Not bad—by the current standards, she took her place among the full-hipped elect. Though she had puffed in agony at her introduction to corsets, she wore them as a priest his dickey—devoutly. Yet none of these charms struck her now as so precious as her teeth, and she thanked her stars she had been smart enough to do what she had done a month before.

That act, had she but known it, she might have traced back to her earliest childhood, to a midget crawling on a cabin floor and betimes staring up at a crone thrusting skeleton fingers toward the fire. The old woman was a yellow mummy, but in the cadaverous head where the skin yawned away from the corners of the mouth, glowed one object of eternal fascination to the child on the floor. Cora watched her grandmother's hand waver upward to the lips; the stick with its teat of wet snuff came away; a yank, and thumb and forefinger brandished in the firelight the sceptre of distinction. The child's eyes were moons, her chubby hands reached vainly, while the hag rocked and cackled. The only gold tooth in the county! To inspect it people had come from as far as Garner's Creek, and the old woman had pulled it out for them and put it back and laughed vaingloriously.

Cora had not thought of her grandmother in years when Tedder projected her into a new world. She was not thinking consciously of her grandmother on that day she flabbergasted a Peachburg dentist by sailing into his parlours and ordering him to jerk out sound molars and replace them with tusks of eighteen karat. Even afterward (sitting as now before her mirror), when she caressed her throbbing jaw, bared her lips and touched with thumb and forefinger the ensanguined glitter, the gesture brought back no recollection. Her heart was too full of the assurance that at last she flaunted the true banner of quality.

There she had what it took to convince a gentleman. Whatever the shade of her hair, whatever the contour of her bust, Major Archibald Waveroon must recognize and pay homage to a lady when, subtly but with intent, that lady smiled. Cora practised the smile while she dressed.

She pulled on the evening stockings, too gorgeous, in her estimation, to be forgone by day. There was a run in one, for her wardrobe had not been lately replenished. She did not mind that, however, as she stroked the pink bulges above her boots of black patent leather with their red kid tops. What was a run or so alongside such splendour? The corset was not so agreeable—she groaned a little—but the green silk petticoat restored her complacence, and the purple suit and the Merry Widow hat with the red plumes, and the striped parasol, sealed it. She tried on her blue beads but decided they clashed; the swastika lavalliere was better. So, with a final dip in the rouge pot and a final squeeze of the atomizer, Cora tucked the parasol under one arm and gave her reflection an iridescent farewell. ...

The lobby of the New York Hotel was a tranquil place in the forenoon, but even the most venerable chairwarmer stirred as Miss LaMont swept by. ...

Major Archibald Waveroon, immaculate from the part in his white toupee to the sheen of his gaiters, sat with hands clasped across his waistcoat inside the plate-glass window of the establishment of which he was owner, manager and—to quote his own fluted advertisements—"uniquely understanding heart." It was the noon hour. Many pedestrians passed and when one of them bowed, the Major inclined his goatee, squinted his eyes and unsquinted them. The restraint of his greeting, which did not vary by a whisker's quiver for this friend or that, seemed to say, "Grin if you will, wave, hulloo, but do not expect me to grin or wave; it would not be fitting here. At the club tonight—ah! we shall see." No rebuke was in his manner, only dignity, tinged with the aura of well- bred grief.

So, at noon yesterday and noon the day before and at many other noons, you would have seen the Major, white toupee and white moustache and white gardenia a part of the window-dressing as becoming as the silver urn on the window-seat. Hurrying Peachburgians were accustomed to the picture he made—accustomed yet withal pleased and a trifle awed by each new beholding. The Major's presence gave them the same glow of pride in their city that the Episcopal cathedral did. For the Major and his establishment were a landmark in Peachburg, one in which all citizens might feel a righteous share. Only the oldest inhabitants could recall when there was no Waveroon's, only the poorest and the Catholics failed to patronize it. The latter took their scanty dead to Mulcahey, the former to J. P. Gibson, whose cut-rate cards in the street cars shocked all but the impecunious devoid of common sensibilities. Nice people buried via Waveroon's or risked the stigma of insulting the deceased.

The Major was a bachelor. Women adored him for his uniquely understanding heart. Men, too, heartily liked him. The Major had not fought on the side of the Confederacy in the Civil War. So far as was known, he had fought on no side, his history before coming to Peachburg being something of a puzzle, but the fact of his prosperity since then too undebatable for question. Yet, though other local grandees more or less avoided the war as a topic in the Major's presence, none gainsaid him his title.

He *looked* like a Major. Outside his plateglass shrine—at his club, at lodge meetings or among the politicians who knew him for a power—he had a reputation for joviality and, in a vague way, the name of a gay dog. Why, most men could not say, more especially since this devil's halo ill matched his lugubrious profession. Yet, for all that, certain whispers clung glamourously about him. One never actually got the straight of the stories—were they ever really heard?—but the dash of crimson persisted along with Waveroon's greys and violets.

On this golden October noon, with the boon of life made more precious by every sunshaft mellowing the streets, the passing pedestrians might have conceived the Major to be pondering the mutability of time and the riddle of the soul. In point of fact, he was considering how much to charge for the Tanner funeral. Whatever the Major's wealth—and his real estate holdings alone were reputed to be worth half a million—he was not dolt enough to forget that the prestige of Waveroon's rooted in humanity's zeal to damn the expense in honouring what is no longer human. It was frequently a ticklish business, as in the case of the Tanners, who were poor but proud, how far to go to avoid making them feel they had been robbed yet to give them the satisfaction of decent financial sacrifice for a Tanner corpse.

The Tanner funeral would begin at one o'clock in the chapel. The Major looked at his watch. It was half past twelve. He took out his handkerchief and leaned forward to fleck from the window the ghost of a speck.

At this moment there entered his vista a spectacle that caused his hand to pause and the handkerchief to jerk as though he were about to wave, an unheard-of posture for the Major to assume. What he saw, however, had mesmerized him.

A woman was crossing the street. She held aloft a parasol of green and orange stripes in incontestable contrast to the purple of her suit and the red of her plumed hat. One hand caught up her skirts from the highway so that, with each step, she displayed a flare of petticoat and a leg signalling above boots of black and red. Her hat had dipped to one side and she had, altogether, a decidedly scampish air. In full view of the Major, she paused at the curb, craning up at the numbers on the shop fronts. He had a good look at her. Suddenly, as he was mentally cataloguing her in her only possible pigeonhole, the woman's eyes met his. She bridled at the sight of the watcher so close to her, but, to the watcher's horror, she must have forgiven him his interest, for all at once she opened her mouth and lavished on him a smile that, for width and brilliance, was the most ghastly thing of the kind he had ever encountered. Then, before he could recover from the shock, she crowned it by seizing her skirts with a flourish and entering—Waveroon's!

The Major's first thought was to curse the fate that sent him, every so often, patrons who belonged by mortuary etiquette to J. P. Gibson. They were fools who let their social ambitions run away with them, they were pests whose money he did not want and whose funerals he contrived to set for the early morning or after dark. Yet he must rise and bow, his agitation not lessened by the fact that, at this moment, a barouche deposited before Waveroon's the bereaved Tanners.

"What can I do for you, madam?" demanded the Major, escaping further violence to his sensibilities by not looking at the creature.

"I got a letter. From Rose Mullins..."

Cora stopped, for a startling change had taken place in the old gentleman. He had turned scarlet and one fist doubled as though he were about to strike her. Involuntarily she stepped back. A stumble. A grunt. "Excuse *me!*" gasped Cora. Spinning about, she was aware of black-garbed, sombre-visaged women and men.

Major Waveroon gulped—loudly. Out of the vaulted dusk hurried a young man.

"Show—" began the Major. His feelings again choked him. One hand waved, one other word sputtered—"out!"

The mourners stood aside.

On the corner Cora turned dazedly to the young man who had escorted her there. He dropped her arm and regarded her in a manner half frightened, half delighted.

"You *have* got a nerve!" remarked the young man.

"But I come to see him on business!" cried Cora.

"At the chapel? In that rig? Don't you know the old man don't do no business like that here?"

"Why not? What rig? Ain't that his office? I got a letter to him! What right's he got putting me out that way? I'm going back in there and tell him to go 'way back and sit down!"

"Hold your horses!" The young man was excited but very earnest. "Don't you go bustin' up no funeral. Feller you want to see is Charlie Harper, Room 932, Ajax Building. On your way now, Violet—on your way!"

The young man backed off, still vigilant. It was evident that, to pass him, Cora would have to do combat. He called to her again from the doorway of Waveroon's, "Room 932, Violet—on your way!"

Cora stood uncertainly for a moment. She was realizing for the first time that the old gentleman was an undertaker. Yet this did not explain his extraordinary behaviour. And why did the young man call her Violet?

Had others witnessed the Major's display of bad manners, they, too, would have been puzzled. Only a few people in all Peachburg, in fact, would have guessed the reasons for the

Major's ire and they, possibly for excellent reasons of their own, would never have revealed the secret. But, since both the Major and the secret are no more today, one may tell it here. It is best told, perhaps, with a picture:

One who lived in Peachburg in the 1900's will recall a viaduct swelling across the network of tracks, cinders and coughing locomotives which formed Peachburg's principal eyesore and, at the same time, her principal prosperity, for the railroads "made" the town. At one end of the viaduct, rose out of the mist of foliage the firm grey breast of the courthouse topped by its nipple tower. At the other end was the boys' high school. The olympus of government, the crucible of youth, and the viaduct linking them above the pit of commerce—the picture is an American allegory. But the allegory does not end there. Burrowing from either end of the viaduct where its back split for the underpass, another street led below the fair prospect of domes and spires. That street was short and dark. It was cut in halves by the railroad tracks and was given over to heavy traffic. Drays lumbered down its slope, trucks staggered out of its gloom. Yet the street had houses. The stroller on the viaduct saw only their roofs, only chimney tops and shingles and gravel, now and again a roof slightly higher than the others lifting a window above the viaduct's edge like a great blank eye. The windows were always shut tight and shaded. Sometimes they were barred, but always they were shaded, always shut.

One of the rules of the boys' high school was suspension for the pupil who, at any time, was seen entering the underpass where drays and trucks went freely. But the students of the 1900's were lads of no unrebel spirit. At the noon recess they might have seen, clattering out of that dark mouth, not a beer wagon but a phaeton or a pair of saddle horses whose occupants or riders, as the case might be, caused the most riotous of games to cease. The boys stood still and stared like wild little animals at the jungle fire. The painted ladies passed. Their smiles were inscrutable or contemptuous. One wonders long afterward what other emotions pulsed under the scarlet and the kalsomine. They clattered on toward the city's Central Park, and the boys, brooding curiously over their books that afternoon, at dismissal walked by twos and threes—never singly—across the viaduct past the great, blank eyes of the windows. At the far end, beneath the courthouse dome, the rebels dodged out of the sunshine into the dusky underpass. They followed the tunnel down to the railroad tracks, glancing to right and left at the houses that bore names instead of numbers—"Blanche," "Vera," "The Mansion," "Seminole Club"—and, if one were lucky and the day was fair, at the faces in the windows. Painted faces. Smiles contemptuous or inscrutable. Liquid eyes unutterably dead and unutterably enticing. "Hello, boys!" That weary, mocking drawl. "Hello." Muttered while little knees shook and little hands went hot and moist. There was the woman, once, who came out in stained crimson and borrowed a match. One never forgot the sick thrill of the lending. And that, to be perfectly frank about it, was the adventure complete. One went home to hug secretly for days the fever lit by that dismal swamp. But not until little boys were little boys no longer did greater daring solve the mysteries of Kelso Street.

To the adults of Peachburg there was nothing mysterious about Kelso Street. It was a cancer or a paradise, according to their leanings in these matters—or, as in the minds of most patriots, a necessary evil never to be mentioned in front of one's womenfolk. The very name, Kelso Street, was taboo in decent society in those days. Yet, even to male adults, Kelso Street held a riddle. It did not bother them much, for they were a carnal lot on the whole. But now and again some barroom gossip or preacher of a low order rose to demand: "Who owns Kelso Street?" The most satisfactory answer either ever got was: "Ask Charlie

Harper." And if Charlie Harper added a whit to their enlighten-
ment, Peachburg never heard of it.

Rotund, beaming Charlie Harper! A model for a barber's
advertisement if barbers advertised in the manner of others—
He is Wearing Our Special Shave, Shampoo and Shine for the
Stout—with his Elk's tooth pendant from his gold watch-chain,
with his yellow diamond sparkling in his Ascot tie, with his cigar
at a dominant tilt, with his derby slightly cocked; but nothing
too gaudy, too genial; the garb ever missed vulgarity by several
colours, the smile benevolence by at least three hard creases in
the jaw.

Of an afternoon in Peachburg you would scarcely find
Charlie in the Regent Saloon, though it was all his, from the
rosewood bar to the oil painting of Aphrodite on the back wall.
His barkeeps would be there, no less than eight, skimming the
foam from tall seidels, plunking out the squat bottles, frosting
the juleps, and anon Charlie himself would amble in, to be hailed
by name from twenty tables. But before five o'clock you would do
better to seek Charlie Harper in Room 932, Ajax Building, on the
door of which you would see nothing but the discreet inscrip-
tion, "Landowners, Inc." Yes, he would be there, in the office
which contained nothing but a safe and a typewriter and a chair
or two, the tall filing cabinet and Charlie's desk.

Behind it, this day, was Charlie himself, derbied, cigared,
pomaded. He leaned forward, talking, for he was not alone, and
by the honey and steel of his voice you would know that the sleek
back, there, belonged to one whom Charlie must impress.

"A floozie?" said Charlie Harper. "You bet she's a floozie!
Ain't I tellin' you she's the one that made a sucker outa that
Beulah feller? I knowed her right off the bat. 'I'm Miss LaMont,'
she says. 'Uh-huh,' I says to her, 'and I'm Henry Ward Beecher;
have a seat, Miss Cora Potts.' That floored her. You see, she don't

think nobody can reco'nize her. Why, she don't even know she looks like a chippy! 'Howdydo, Mister Harper, and please to pass the Brussel sprouts,' and her dressed up like Mrs. Astor's horse! That's what surprised her when you throwed her out 'sted of puttin' her in the best pew. Don't worry—she don't know till yet how come. But she ain't such a fool as she looks. I found that out after chewin' the fat a while. And she's got money. That's the ticket. Enough to rent a first-class house—and enough sense to run it, too, with a little help from headquarters."

Charlie's cigar puffed his satisfaction, Charlie's swivel chair creaked to the thrust of his hams.

"Then you're leasing her The Mansion?"

A voice vaguely familiar. Across the desk from Charlie, where has one seen that meticulous part in the white hair, the dapper goatee, the gardenia in the button-hole? Why, Major Waveroon! Who would have expected to find *you* here? But then—one always heard, obscurely, those tales about you.

Chapels where the dead sleep can seem noisier sometimes than the corridors of hotels in the late night. The room where Cora lay was dark save for the opaque oblong of the transom; footfalls that passed were muffled, impersonal, as though feet without bodies made them. In the hushed dark, alone, she made her decision, stripping her mind of the little decencies, going unblushing to the naked facts. That was her way.

The man, Mr. Harper, might not be honest, but he knew much. He had known her the minute he saw her, no getting around that. He was a man to be afraid of, but by the same token a man to tie to. She needed a man like that, a smart man, neither a Tedder nor a Bruce nor an old fool like that Waveroon, to tell her what to do. For she had to do something. No getting around that, either. Money didn't last forever. It was fine to get money, but finer to hold onto what you got and then get more. The spinning mill was better than Catamount. Tedder was better than the spinning mill. This, for all her losses, was better than Tedder, for she was her own woman. But this wasn't enough. For money wasn't all of it, money was just a means. That dim star toward which she strove was what counted. And she was yet so far from it! What was it the man had said?

"This ain't a bad business. You hear a lot of guff. Preachers, reformers—what do they know? Most of the girls wouldn't swap if they could. What would they do if they wasn't in it? Dishwashin', scrubbin', cotton mills maybe. Just as bad or worse if they was married. You ain't no kid. You've seen life, sister. I reckon you think you're pretty smart, don't you? But every girl in this house I'm tellin' you about wears sweller clothes and wears 'em better than what you do. I ain't meanin' to hurt your feelin's. I'm talkin' to you like a friend. You say you don't understand what happened downstairs, huh? You would if you could see yourself like they seen you. You paid a lot for them duds, I reckon, but you don't look right—know what I mean? You don't look right! Don't you go and get huffy, 'cause I'm tellin' you like a friend, but any goof could see with one eye *you* wasn't no lady! But give you two months in The Mansion and I'd bet anybody the drinks you could walk down the main drag and they wouldn't know you from Lillian Russell. Am I right? Besides, the proposition I'm makin' you, you wouldn't be no common woman. Listen—"

And she had listened, cheeks hot from shame, from horror, not at Mr. Harper's proposition, not at the iniquities he so airily sketched, but at the realization that the Merry Widow hat, the purple suit, the striped parasol, were not, somehow, what she had fondly supposed them, that the net result of her months of dreaming and spending and experimenting was to get her kicked out of an undertaking parlour.

So Cora, in the dark, alone, met the naked facts and made her decision untrammelled by the little decencies. She got up after a while and switched on the lights and picked up her clothes from the floor where she had hurled them. The stockings were as soft as ever in her hand, but their caress brought only a lump to her throat now. Snuffling a little, on one of them she wiped her nose.

CHAPTER FOUR
THE MANSION

I N 1910 the American people joined in a curious emotional spree. Yet, though the effect on the national scene rivals prohibition's, you will find the upheaval recorded today only as a footnote to history.

That was the year of Halley's comet, hookworm, the Mad Mullah, the beef probe, Dr. Cook's confession and the death of Mark Twain. In May the princes of the earth, with Theodore Roosevelt's face black from African suns, followed the corpse of Edward Seventh through rain-chilled streets to Westminster Abbey. Glenn Curtiss broke all air records in a hop from Albany to New York, and across a Florida beach Barney Oldfield was a roaring phantom at 133 miles an hour, "the fastest man has ever travelled." While Paris hailed the discovery of antityphoid vaccine, eighteen thousand howling whites at Reno, Nevada, watched a black man slug the hope of their race. A little later twenty Negroes were lynched at Palestine, Texas, suffragettes broke the windows of Parliament, England hanged Dr. Crippen, and Tolstoy and Mary Baker Eddy went to their rewards. But, by the time children were whisking up chimneys letters demanding Teddy bears from Santa Claus, America had forgotten kings and comets for one absorbing tocsin. Eight states had passed "white slave" acts, and the other forty were fast swinging into line before a hydra that stalked wherever mothers and daughters breathed.

A few years before, vice had basked. No city that could muster a militia battalion but sheltered its red light beyond the river or back of the yards. Then—in a rented room over a Chicago saloon a woman burst into maudlin tears. Her identity is forgotten, but not the note she dropped from the window in a megalomania induced by drugs and whisky. A serious young milkman picked up the scrawl, took it to a young assistant district attorney, not so serious but shrewdly ambitious. When the coppers came, a puzzled barkeep willingly led them up and watched while beauty in distress clawed her rescuers. But by then ambition had struck hands with the press, and the pebble was bounding toward the avalanche. For the note had contained a phrase jogged out of heaven-knows-what nook of memory in that fuddled brain. ... "I am a white slave." ...

So the ogreish legend was born. The Chicago Vice Commission began investigations in a welter of sensation. In New York, brawling over Tammany, rebels pounced on a new red flag to brandish at the politicians; a special grand jury met with a Baptist multimillionaire for a foreman. Reformers elsewhere were not to be outdone. Yellow journalism, at its lustiest, shattered its limits. Muckraking magazines, tottering, hailed a new lease on life. The conservatives wobbled once and surrendered to the last grisly detail. In a single year famous old "Leslie's Weekly" published twenty-five articles on white slavery. "The House of Bondage" exploded on the book counters one October and by Spring was outselling "The Rosary." In brief, prostitution was served with the morning coffee in thirty million homes, and though, before many weeks, an asylum in Pennsylvania sheltered a fifteen-year-old virgin babbling of poison needles and oily foreigners, nothing could stop the tidal wave of righteousness. Where a constitutional amendment outlawed demon rum in America, the red light was slain by almost as many ordinances as there were townships—and slain swiftly, universally, utterly. Never has "public sentiment" won such a moral victory in the United States without a civil war.

Down with the national bogey went a national saga. The sinful old legends, the sinful old speech, the Don Juans and the Circes and the notorious seraglios of their heyday, these are scarcely names to a new generation that never heard of Rose Bailey's, thinks Frankie was a waitress and Johnny a cowboy, regards the Barbary Coast as a place the movies invented, and believes the Ever-leigh Club was something like the Union League. All vastly wicked, no doubt, and the world is better off without them. Only wicked old men would dream, for an instant, that a sturdiness and a lustre passed with them, too.

The city of Peachburg, like every other city before the great crusades, had its legends. In 1910 these concerned principally a house known as The Mansion and its mistress, Thelma LaMont. Men said that the paintings in The Mansion were old masters imported from Europe. Its rooms were walled with mirrors and in some rooms mirrors were the ceilings. Nothing but champagne was served in The Mansion. Its ballroom contained no automatic piano but a six-piece orchestra under a "professor" who had played for crowned heads in his day. It cost five dollars to get in the front door of The Mansion and nothing less than fifty to get out, and even then you must be a person of social consequence or an alderman.

Most of the legends were recited by gentlemen, who, if pressed, would admit they had not personally visited The Mansion but were friends of gentlemen who had and who vouched roundly for the truth of the stories.

Thelma LaMont, said the gentlemen, was more beautiful than Venus and more passionate than tigers. She was, of course, marvellously educated. Some said she was the divorced wife of a United States Senator, others that she was the bastard daughter of a celebrated diva. Among the local college boys it was gospel that Thelma was a graduate of Vassar and a nymphomaniac. A bishop's son swore she had lain with him and confided her life's story. She had, said he, quoted Swinburne as off-handedly as that.

Curtis Rowlett, a reporter for the Peachburg Star and Register, claimed to know as much about Thelma LaMont as anyone. He could be found almost any night kicking his heels and swapping yarns with the call officers at police headquarters, or, as on this day, somewhere in the vicinity. He had walked two blocks west from the station-house, crossed the railroad tracks and entered the gloom that was Kelso Street, carrying a thickness of newspapers under his arm and whistling "The Trail of the Lonesome Pine." At the end of the street, before the most pretentious of the houses, he stopped and pulled the old-fashioned door bell. It was noon of a hot Sunday in June and something less than nine years from the day that Cora Potts shinned over the window-sill of her father's store to trudge her dusty road from Catamount to the world.

Three women were having breakfast in the kitchen of The Mansion. They sat around a table covered by a stained oil-cloth while a coloured girl sweated in a blue cloud over a stove in the corner. Neither about them nor their surroundings was there anything splendid or romantic. Yet the scene was not without a certain homely cheer. The sputter of grease and the gabble of the women were pleasant sounds, and the sunshine was pleasant on crockery, peeling walls and the fly-specked Coca-Cola calendar.

There entered Carmen, lighting a cigarette butt. In a wrapper, with her hair knotted back and her gaunt face bare of rouge, she was no enchantress. But authority sat on that horsey jaw, bitter humour in the eyes. A topsergeant of marines. A boss blacksmith in a trade where men were so many horses to be shod. She flopped into a chair.

"Gawd, what a night! If many more of them Shriners holds their conventions in this joint I'm gonna join the Elks. Pour me a drink, Zebby. Nothin' like the hair of the dog that bit you."

"Mis' Thelma she say the ladies ain't to have no whisky 'lessen one of the gem'mems buys it."

The Negro proceeded serenely with the frying of eggs.

"Miss Thelma can kiss my foot. Ain' I the housekeeper? I want a drink, and a hackman's peg, too."

Hazel, a peroxide blonde, interceded across the table. Hers were the pale eyes of a usurer, but in the house she was noted for her "crying jags." On slight provocation, she wept to be back in Buford, Georgia, at blossom time.

"Don't be nasty, Carmen. You know Miss Thelma'd fire Zebby right out of here if she caught her in the whisky. We got regular old-time waffles this mawnin'."

"Who's nasty? Zebby makes me gag. She's gettin' as biggety as Thelma herself—'no whisky for the ladies!' ... No whisky for the whores, you mean. Gimme a bottle of beer then, Zebby."

Lilyan, a tall brunette, left off polishing her nails to give a click of disgust.

While Zebby served the beer, Carmen glowered.

"Who asked you to butt in, Sitting Bull? Go take a ride on your bottom. I said 'whores' and I don't care how many ancestors you got back in Charleston—that's what you are. ... Thanks, honey."

The fourth prostitute, May, was really a pretty girl, younger than the others and given to vacant laughter. During the wrangle she had been emitting titters to which the rest paid no attention. Now, passing Carmen the salt, she tittered again at Hazel's warning—"Don't spill it, give you seven years' bad luck, dearie."

Lilyan yawned.

"Really, though—beer at breakfast! All I've got to say is I'm glad I haven't the opinion some folks have of their- self. Miss LaMont never treated *me* like anything but a lady."

"She never, huh? Try and hold out on her sometime. I saw her claw a girl wide open over six bits. What I want to know is—where'd she get the latest—that sharp-shooter's medal she had on last night?"

"You mean the cameo pin, my dear? It's a family heirloom, she told me."

"Well, it's the first time I ever heard of anybody leavin' their family heirlooms in a sportin' house."

At this added piece of vulgarity Lilyan rose. Carmen drained her beer.

"Goin', Lady Thundermug? Give my love to the Duke. You better take him up a bromo. When I passed the palace comin' down, he was groanin' like all forty. Your Ladyship musta kicked him out of bed."

Carmen winked at the other girls as Lilyan slammed the door.

"She's all right. Only she thinks hustlin' is a lawn-party. Swell—if you can get away with it. Now you take Thelma, she never misses a trick. Hard as hell in the house. Handles drunks bare-handed and don't muff a dime. But outside? Say, you meet Thelma on the main drag and you'd never give her a tumble. Don't try to, either, if you know what's healthy."

Carmen mopped her plate with a waffle.

"Thelma," she continued, "has got the dough, the first nickel she ever made and then some. And Thelma's got the class. Where the hell she got it, you can search me, but she can wrastle Lilyan all over the place when it comes to class. That dame spits like a lady!"

"Her folks musta been somebody," remarked Hazel.

"Uh-huh, like frawgs musta been tad-poles. Say, I've known Thelma—well, longer'n anybody around this dump, and some day when you get me drunk enough, dearie, I'll give you the works. It won't be any Blue Book, neither. Naw, Thelma's changed. Why, when I first knew her she'd no more of wore that sharp-shooter's whatsit than she'd of slept with a nigger. But now she thinks it's class—see?"

At this moment the door-bell rang, and Zebby shuffled off to answer it.

Curtis Rowlett nodded airily.

"Hello, Zebby. Miss Thelma here?"

"Ah'll see."

He waited in the hallway while the Negro disappeared abovestairs. He stood with his feet wide apart on the red carpet, his hands in his pockets, his cap still on his head. A stranger here might have looked about him, at the brocade curtains, at the pictures, at the marble Aphrodite, the palms, the treasures of The Mansion of which he had heard so much. Curtis Rowlett looked at none of these things. He whistled "The Trail of the Lonesome Pine," and he looked at his shoes, which were yellow and highly polished. When he took out a cigarette and lit it, the movement necessitated a dislodgment of his papers. This seemed to bring a very agreeable thought to his mind, for he laughed—a short, loud snort of a laugh, like the bark of a small dog trying to imitate a big dog.

Kee-rist! What a lot of saps they were at the office. He always knew that big piece of cheese, Swanson, would pull a bobble sooner or later. Call that sap a reporter! Well, he hoped Swanson got it in the pants. Teach them to appreciate a man with brains. Now if they'd shown him that picture ... If he'd been Swanson. ... Or Wes Russell, the managing editor ... But no, they stuck a guy with brains on a dirty police run where he had to 'phone in all his stuff. Fifteen dollars a week and rot your life away on a lotta dopes and bulls. If he'd been Swanson … but Swanson had a college education. A rah-rah boy. Kee-rist, what he knew about rah-rah boys! God damn snobs. Why, in this house last week, when that frat gang from Polytech got drunk. … And their damn pins in every pawnshop on Bartow Street. … Besides, he could have gone to college himself if he'd wanted to, couldn't he? Sure he could. The old man had been wild to send him to theology school. But he was too smart for a come-on like that. A preacher!—can you beat it? Why, he was wise to more stuff than all the preachers in this town. Real stuff—the paper, politics, what Chief Palmer was telling him only last night, and women like Thelma LaMont anxious to stand in with him; in a way, you know, he was a power in this town. If he only had money! He'd seen right off the bat there was no money in preaching. Not that fifteen dollars a week and rot your life away was so good. They'd have to come across with him on the paper before long. Or else he'd get out. Into a good press-agent job, into business maybe. Now you take the patent-medicine business. A gold mine! He knew a trick or two about that. He had his eye out for whatever came along. You bet he did! Well, let 'em wait. …

"Miss Thelma say you come on up."

Curtis Rowlett in the hallway of The Mansion, feet apart, cap on the back of his head, tossed away his cigarette, stopped whistling "The Trail of the Lonesome Pine," and went abovestairs.

A fit of restlessness, unusual for her, bothered the mistress of The Mansion. As a rule her Sundays were given to finance. The safe was opened, accounts carefully ordered, her door kept locked against everyone but Zebby. And the safe was open now. So was her "secretary." Papers and money littered its drop-leaf. But Thelma stood at the window, letting the sun pour against her face and neck and bosom. A moment before she was at the mirror, where for some time she had been gazing, without movement, at her reflection. And before that she had been circling, circling about the room.

The room was not unpleasant. A combination of parlour and bed-chamber. Rose drapes at the window. Rose drapes over the four-poster bed. A rose lamp beside the chaise-longue with its rose upholstering and its lacy pillows. The rug on the floor was of a deeper rose than the rest. When the drapes were drawn, the lamp lit, the room shut tight against all air but its own—and this would be attar of roses, insufferably sweet—one imagined the room closed about him as the petals of a huge, tropical rose might suddenly garrote a curious insect.

But the room, like the motes in silent collision in the sunshine above the deep rose rug, warred with itself. The "secretary," an old American piece, frowned at the chaise-longue. The four-poster frowned at the cherubs carved over the vanity dresser. Pictures clashed. You could pick the original settlers from the newer ones—Harrison Fisher girls, their passe-partout frames peeling, from the Countess Potocka in elaborate gilt. A copy of "September Morn" from a dry-point etching of Notre Dame. So with the magazines on the console table—"Snappy Stories," "The Ladies' Home Journal," "Jim- Jam-Jems," "House and Garden." And the books above the "secretary"—"Etiquette in 20 Lessons," "The Common Law," "The Song of the Yukon," Spalding's Baseball Guide, three volumes on book-keeping and banking from the International Correspondence School, "Life's Shop-Window" by Victoria Cross, "The Complete Letter Writer" and two books by Dr. Orison Swett Marden, "The Power of Personality" and "Good Manners and Success"—this was the library of the landlady of The Mansion.

The landlady of The Mansion ... you have seen her, barefoot, the little savage destined to the hoe, the furrow and the sun;

brushed out of nowhere by her own dishonesty and a seducer abetted by the music of the Lord; looking up from her Bucktown dungheap to a far star, one sofa pillow, "O You Kid!"; lifted into a paradise of licorice drops, sen-sen and sin, only to be hurled down into jail and odium; valiantly resolving to make the best of calamity and the five thousand she salvaged; then pondering her entry into a profession which, however reprehensible to the right-minded today, could still enlist the cupidity of pillars of society at the time Cora Potts changed her name to Thelma LaMont. Seven years of that profession obviously have prospered her. But because they are the details of any successful commercial enterprise, let us skip the mechanics of exactly how Cora became the madam of Peachburg's most exclusive resort to examine, in Thelma, what she became.

"In five years," Charlie Harper had said, "they won't be able to tell you from Mrs. Astor." It was no fatuous prediction. As Carmen said, had you met Thelma on the main drag, you would have expected Peachburg's finest to bow to her. Many, indeed, almost did—and caught back the nod with a throb of terror that Thelma would return it. But she, a wiser woman than the novice who blundered into Waveroon's, passed on as cool as a glacier. Whereupon, perhaps, a gentleman's lady remarked to a gentle-man, "Did you see that marvellous leopardskin coat—I wonder who she is?" The ladies' gentlemen never knew.

Even here, in a cloister where the trappings of the world are of no avail, Thelma bears well the scrutiny that would brand her other than a respectable member of society. She had discarded, in the third year of her rule, the ball-gown for day wear. She is crisply dressed in linen. Her arms are bare to the elbow. Her throat is open. The flesh revealed is plump, but white and clean. Where is the unwashed hair of the Catamount brat? Where the beads of Tedder's woman? The splotches? The ranks of gold teeth? Thelma's hair, which has known more hues than one in these seven years, has settled to an uncertain brown. But it is soft and wavy. The gold teeth vanished, one day, as violently as they came. A mole decorates one forearm—that is all. As for ornament, though diamonds and pearls shimmer beneath the lid of that box on the dresser, Thelma LaMont displays one splendour. It sleeps at the pit of her neckline, between her ample breasts, sardonyx and old gold the size of a soup-spoon, the "family heirloom," the cameo pin.

It is this she has been studying before her mirror, fingering the relief work, changing the pin's position, trying it suspended from a long black ribbon—at last letting it rest, staring at it in the mirror as once she stared at the sofa pillow among the canes, the watches and the knives.

Zebby had to knock twice. When the coloured woman went out and Thelma turned to the window and pulled back the drapes, you would have noticed two details not included in a previous appraisal. The mistress of The Mansion, after all, was no more perfect than her quarrelling room. On her feet, under the crisp linen, blazed French slippers of pink with high green heels. And her occupation was not drinking in the sunshine as she stood there; she was sousing herself with attar of roses.

"Hi!" said Curtis Rowlett, out of the side of his mouth, an effect designed to indicate masterful ease.

Thelma was busy with the atomizer. Curtis Rowlett, as he himself might have put it, was no treat to her. Since police headquarters was but two blocks from the district and Curtis had an arrangement with the desk sergeant in case of murder, fire or a call from the office, he was able to spend a good part of his time around the houses. To chat with the girls and cadge drinks from the madams, made him feel the hellrake. At his office he was regarded not only as an authority on vice but as the lover of half a dozen notorious wantons, a role he was at some care to foster. Actually Curtis was both too poor and too timorous to be the Don Juan he played. His sordid little "affairs" were mainly pumped out of what he saw and heard. Thelma tolerated him because he could be useful to her with the police and because he brought her the gossip of the town. She even liked him. He was eager to please and a little afraid of her, and he had a certain hard cunning which she appreciated.

"Well, how's tricks?" she asked, locking the safe. "Saint Luke raided any more nigger crap games?"

The reference was to the new chief of police, Luke Palmer, an honest man and a Baptist deacon, who had startled even the "reform" faction that elected him by a war on the city's gambling houses, thus far with only negligible results because of the willingness of Chief Palmer's subordinates to take bribes from the gentlemen on whom he sicked them.

Curtis had swaggered to a chair and lit a cigarette. He extended his legs leisurely, for he was yet young enough to feel gusto at the mere fact of his presence in a house of ill-fame. His usual awe of Thelma seemed less today, and she noticed this with the conclusion that something was up.

"Oh, the chief's all right," said Curtis. "Just a big sap. He don't know whether Christ was crucified or killed by the Indians, but he means well. Know what he told me last night? But that ain't what I came for. Wanted to show you something. This is gonna hand you a laugh."

The thickness of newspapers unfolded. Thelma, from the chaise-longue, received the page Curtis handed her. Her face was invisible behind the uplifted sheet as he rattled on.

"Ain't it a beaut? 'Prominent Society Woman at Dog Show'— Kee-rist! If the paper ever hears the last of this!—Say, Thelma, do you know you've sprung the prize laugh of the season on the little old Star-Register? I can see Marcellus P.'s face this minute! And what he won't do to Wes Russell and Swanson—oh, boy!"

Curtis, his head thrown back, cackled.

"What's so funny?" said Thelma, and she lowered the paper. He looked at her open-mouthed, at her cold light eyes, at her unsmiling lips, and his own lips slopped.

"Why, don't you see? The joke on the Star-Register—printing your picture like you were a real society dame."

Across the smudge in her lap Thelma studied him.

"No, I don't see. It's not the first picture they ever printed, is it?"

"Well, I reckon it's the first time they ever printed a picture of a—of a—see here, how come they got the picture? How come you went to the dog show?"

"Because I wanted a dog," said Thelma, simply. Curtis fidgeted.

"I wanted to buy a dog," she went on, "and I did buy one. It was a prize dog, one of those little ones. They're very swell, you know. I was sticking it up my sleeve to see how cute it looked, when the man came along and took my picture. I didn't ask him to. I didn't tell him I was a society woman, neither. He just took it and he asked me what my name was, and I told him it was Mrs. Potter, and he wrote it down. I suppose it is kind of funny."

It could never be said of Curtis Rowlett, however suspect his actions either as a reporter or in those later years of grandeur, that he was not a man of perception. Or that, having perceived, he was laggard to trim his sails to the wind's veer. And he perceived now that Thelma LaMont, unaccountable though it was, did not think it funny for her picture to be in the paper as a "prominent society woman's."

Curtis frowned. "Well, now, I don't say as it's so awfully funny—except to somebody on the inside. Fellers on the paper, fellers around town. Come to think about it, I don't know as I blame Swanson so much. Most anybody might take you for a society dame, Thelma."

"Would they?" said Thelma. She no longer looked at Curtis, but with her fingers smoothed the paper across her knee. And he was aware of both a sneer and a wistfulness behind her question, and of the smell of her and of the toes of her slippers leering up along the silken tracks of her calves. Curtis laughed nervously.

"Why, sure they would!" he protested. "Sure!"

Thelma kept on smoothing the paper and wrinkling up the toes of the pink slippers with their high, green heels.

"Do you know, Curtis," she said finally, "I'd like to get out of this business. I'd like to get into something that would make me as much money and still be—well, kind of respectable."

Curtis Rowlett's left eye twitched, a habit he had when he was excited or afraid.

"Say, Thelma, you've got the right idea. Now you take the patent medicine business—there's a gold mine! Why, I know an old nigger down here back of Bucktown that's cleaning up with stuff he sells to other niggers. I been talking to him and he'll sell me his formula for two hundred dollars. Why, if I had that formula I bet you inside a year I'd be worth twenty thousand. Listen, Thelma, why don't you and me—"

But Thelma was paying no attention. She had turned a page of the newspaper as Curtis became enthusiastic, and from simple indifference she had gone on to complete insensibility to him. Out of the paper yawned an advertisement, page wide and page deep, a gorilla and a girl, huge paws throttling her nude to its hairy breast, teeth slavering, eyes insane, boxcar letters, and columns, columns—her own name—

"Listen, Thelma—"

She whirled on him with a screech. "Shut up, you fool! Look at this! Who's responsible for this? I'll kill him! I'll have the law on him! What sort of a God-damn paper is this—printing a lot of dirty stink about me? Ruining my business! Calling me—calling me—"

She choked, balled the paper between clenched nails, heaved from the chaise-longue, and charged across the room, green heels clattering.

"Zebby! Carmen!"

Curtis goggled at the torn shreds of girl and gorilla:

"The White Slave in Our Midst!—Art Thou Thy Sister's Keeper?—Know Thyself, Man!—Know Thyself, Peachburg!—The Red Light Must Go!"

A name caught his eye.

"Aw, Thelma, it ain't nobody but that fool preacher, Harris. Why, listen, Thelma—"

Thelma was no longer there. Below, he could hear her heels, diminuendo, on the stairs. Curtis sighed, cocked his cap on the side of his head, lit a cigarette and strolled out.

First, however, he "borrowed" five dollars from the money scattered on the "secretary." More was there, but Curtis lacked a great deal of courage.

CHAPTER FIVE
CRUSADE

"AND SO," concluded Thelma, bitterly,—"I gotta sit still and do nothin' while my business goes bang, just because a big-mouth preacher calls my girls 'white slaves'—and not one of 'em would swap places with a preacher's punk tomorrow!"

"Well, sister," admitted Charlie Harper, "you ain't far wrong. I wouldn't worry if it wasn't for Chief Palmer. The Mayor's all right. They can't scare him. But Luke Palmer may not wait for the Mayor's say-so. He can crack down whenever he's a mind to."

"The hell he can!"

"The hell he can't. The law says nix on disorderly houses, and nobody claims Kelso Street's a ladies' seminary. What do you think you been payin' the Lieutenant two hundred a month for—charity? If this Harris gets to the Chief hard enough, it's Katy bar the door. The chief's got a conscience."

Thelma groaned. Preachers and consciences she had learned to distrust long ago on a Sunday afternoon in Caneyville, when they joined in her betrayal. As she left Charlie Harper's office, it would have gone hard with the Reverend Jethro Harris had she encountered him between the door and her Pierce-Arrow.

Reverend Jethro Harris was pastor of the Rock Street Baptist Tabernacle, boasting the largest if not the most select congregation in Peachburg. He was also president of the newly formed Christ and Purity League, backed by the millions of old Isaac

Crane. The Christ and Purity League had rammed prohibition down the state's throat five years before, greatly to the profit of the Crane candy and soft drink interests. Now, largely as a reward to Jethro for doubling the sales of Krane-Ko-Pop, old Isaac was paying for those gorilla advertisements. They were raw meat for a community which had barred "Three Weeks" from its library and Evelyn Nesbit from its stage, whose newspapers had a standing rule against the use of the word "adultery" except in quoting Scripture, and whose department stores refused to advertise corsets with pictures of undressed ladies. But because the crusade was waged in the name of holy church, the newspapers accepted the gorillas and the community gobbled them with relish, particularly the young boys and young girls whose souls were saved thereby.

It was the Sunday afternoon custom of Reverend Jethro Harris, after his effort of the morning and to gird him for the evening labours, to take a nap. The children were banished to neighbours, Mrs. Harris retired, and Jethro lay down on the black leather couch in his study, whence usually his snores assured his wife that she might pursue her guilty sewing in peace. Jethro's effort this morning had been unusual, the open charge that the police department was in league with the red light, and his plans for the night called for even greater histrionics, no less than the presentation in his pulpit of a "white slave." She was Carrie Todhunter, a half-starved country girl whom the police had picked up on the streets for soliciting and sent to the Mary and Martha Home. Jethro, ranging there for a purpose and failing to lasso any of the other inmates, had browbeaten her into volunteering for his tableau by his insistence that thus only could she escape damnation. She was not pretty, but perhaps, Jethro was thinking, the fact was just as well, her boniness would enhance the realism of the paper chains he proposed to dangle around her. At the proper moment Jethro would strike them off, where-upon the members of the Philathea class would advance down the aisle singing "Whiter Than Snow," and enfold the lost sheep to their bosoms. The Philatheas were to wear robes and carry crosses, a touch Jethro dared in the face of a qualm that it would offend some of the more sanguinary Catholic-baiters in his flock. He, too, had a proper hatred of the Pope, but he did like a crack-ing good show.

Despite the tilting ahead of him and behind him, Jethro did not sleep. He lay on his back, staring with his pop eyes at an engraving of the boy Jesus teaching in the temple, and though the hot day and the drawn blinds made perspiration bead on Jethro's nose, he did not twitch. Jethro was absorbed in schem-ing tactics. His ability to prime the second gun before he had fired the first, had boosted him from a backwoods revival tent to the city and was destined, he knew, to carry him much far-ther. He was still in the rapids of the prohibition adventure when he mapped out his sermons on the dance evil. He was still lam-basting the turkey trot and the bunny hug when he pounced on mixed bathing in, the municipal swimming pool. City council was still hearing from him on that subject when he personally toured the movie theatres and caught two girls smoking in an exit. And mothers were still marching their daughters from these lairs of lust when Jethro sat in old Isaac Crane's library, reading him the reports of the Rockefeller grand jury on organized vice in New York. So now, though Carrie Todhunter was yet to be saved publicly, Jethro was a week ahead of the morrow's head-line, gnawing his brain for the idea that would land him on the front page the following Monday. As yet he had hit on none. He wondered if it would help to pray a little.

Jethro, his enemies to the contrary, was no hypocrite. When a whisky lobbyist sneered at him for a four-flushing reformer during the prohibition battle and Jethro, drawing himself up to his full height, thundered, "Sir, I am the sword of God!" he believed it. So, when he prayed, it was with confidence that the ear of God was exclusively his, and results had justified this assurance. Had not Jethro, on his nuptial night, gotten down on his knees in his nightshirt and prayed that it would be a boy? And had not the Lord in due time answered his prayer? Praying in his study this hot Sunday afternoon for an idea that would make a good story for the papers, Jethro was in earnest. Nor was he surprised, in the midst of his prayer, to hear the door-bell ring. The Lord's hand was ever prompt.

Jethro got up from his knees and went in person to receive his caller.

Curtis Rowlett had no notion that he was about to be greeted as the answer to a prayer. His city editor had sent him to ask Jethro whether he had any real dope to back up that stuff about police graft, and Curtis, what with a reporter's natural contempt for preachers and his leanings toward his police pals who had been attacked, waited belligerently on the Harris stoop.

"Come in, my boy," beamed Jethro. "Ah—how is your father?"

He had recognized Curtis not only as one of his friends of the press but as the son of a minister—a Baptist minister at that. Curtis, swaggering into the study, pretended not to hear. The query annoyed him, since it presumed a tie between himself and a person to whom he felt superior.

"My paper," he plunged at once, "wants to know more about those charges you made this morning. All that holler about the police takin' money to protect the bawdy houses."

Jethro waved to a chair. Conciliation was always his tack with his friends of the press, and he prided himself on his ability to talk as man to man, calling spades spades.

"Just what is it your paper wishes to know, my boy?"

"Why, how true they are, how much evidence you got. Whether you can give names and figures or"—Curtis wavered between reportorial diplomacy and the impulse to take another crack at Jethro—"whether you was just shootin' off your mouth?"

Jethro frowned. The young man was determined to be trying.

"Mr. Rowlett," and he fixed Curtis with his eyes and put thumb to thumb, "I am not in the habit of making false or rash statements. You, as a trained journalist, are familiar with the laws of libel." Curtis was no trained journalist and he had but the baldest notion of the laws of libel, but the assumptions pleased him. "You are aware that, on the basis of my assertions today, I could be sued. I would have to prove my assertions in court or pay heavy damages. I will not be sued, Mr. Rowlett. And I will prove them."

Jethro paused to give every word significance.

"Mr. Rowlett, I would like to give you the data in my possession. I would like to give the story to the Star- Register. It is a good paper. I would like to give you the story, for I admire your talent. But I cannot. Circumstances, my committee, bind me to wait. However, by next Sunday I promise you I will make public documents—proofs—facts—that will shake this city."

Jethro glanced at his desk, which at once took on the colour of a repository of criminal secrets.

"Ah, young man, if you had the faintest conception of the cesspools of vice around us, you would shudder. You would shudder, young man, if I told you a tithe of what I know—aye, one single story of the hundreds I have on record! You would say, 'You exaggerate; such things cannot be in Peachburg!' "

If Jethro's purpose was to horrify as well as conciliate his interviewer, he was shooting wide of the mark. Curtis had been mollified by the clerical unction, but the charge that he was an innocent was too much.

"Say, Doctor Harris, you can't tell me nothin' about vice in Peachburg. Why, I could tell you stuff that would knock your eye out!"

Jethro had forgotten he was not addressing a congregation. He blinked.

"Surest thing you know," continued Curtis. "Why, I reckon I know more about vice in Peachburg than you could learn in ten years. There ain't many in this man's town know Kelso Street like I do. Inside and out, forwards and backwards. 'Course it's my business to know such things. But if you think you could make me shudder—shucks, I wrote the book!"

The youth tilted back.

"Not that I'm goin' to slip you the office on anything. I ain't no stool pigeon. Just the same, I reckon you'd be surprised if you knew where I was less'n an hour ago. No harm tellin' you. The Mansion! Know what that is? That's Thelma LaMont's house!"

"That wicked woman!"

The words burst unstudied from Jethro.

"Aw, she ain't so wicked. Thelma's a good skate when you get to know her. 'Course if she don't like you"—he chuckled—"gosh, if you'd heard her today! Cuss? She wrote the book! She was cussin' you, too."

"But I would not knowingly hurt one of those unfortunate creatures."

Curtis stared. "Ain't you goin' kinder strong after that little piece in the paper, Doc? The one about the monkey and all that stuff. You don't think Thelma LaMont was exactly tickled by that, do you?"

"If I named her, it was because she had become a symbol of the plague tearing at our community's vitals. Besides, if I remember right, the language along there was pretty careful. I invited her to put away her life of shame and atone for her sins—to close her place, in short."

"Close her place? She'd rather lose an eye."

" 'Though thy sins be as—' "

"I know, I know! You can't tell me nothin' about the Bible. I know the Bible forwards and backwards. But that ain't the point. Come to think about it, you might get her."

He stopped.

"Yes?" inquired Jethro.

"Nothin'. I ain't no stool pigeon. But keep your eye on Thelma, Doc. She don't hanker to run a house so much as some folks think. I know. I'm on the inside around here. You go on save her, Doc! Maybe you can."

Curtis barked his dog's laugh.

But Jethro did not smile. He was suddenly abstracted.

In truth, Jethro forgot Curtis with the closing of the door. He made haste to his study and there resumed his flat position. But only for a few minutes. His eyes snapped, he sat up, he popped his fingers like a crapshooter.

"I've got it, Lord!" he shouted.

That night, in Rock Street Church, the people shivered on the edge of frenzy as the Philatheas burst wailing through the doors and the paper chains spilled about Carrie Todhunter's ankles. Women leaped up to praise the Lord, men sobbed, and Jethro knew he had once more rung the bell. Monday's papers gave him his due; Tuesday the gorilla charged again above harrowing columns; Tuesday afternoon certain patroons of the city met, smoked many cigars and agreed, as Major Waveroon put it, there was nothing to do save let the dervish whirl his course. And in Wednesday's dawn, propping a chair against the doorknob of her room in The Mansion, May, the pretty prostitute, dissolved six tablets of bichloride of mercury and gulped the dose.

Ordinarily a suicide in Kelso Street drew scanty treatment in the Peachburg dailies. The thing was among the banned, first-family divorces and department-store accidents. Without knowing exactly why, reporters and copy readers yet knew the death must take a stick on the market page. But the Christ and Purity League, buyers of space, was under no such compulsion. Jethro seized the gift from heaven at full stride.

"Thou Art the Man!" the box-car letters shrieked. "At sunrise yesterday, while a great city condoned the murder, the Beast in Our Midst struck. The blood of the young girl who killed herself in the Red Light's maw is not on her own head; it is wet on the hands of our public officials and on the hands of every citizen who says, by his silence, 'I AM THE FRIEND OF THE BEAST; I APPROVE THE DEBAUCHERY OF SOUTHERN WOMANHOOD AND THE RUIN OF YOUNG MANHOOD; THROW OUR GIRLS TO THE BROTHEL AND OUR BOYS TO THE JUNGLE! AM I MY BROTHER'S KEEPER?' "

Thelma read and spat, a thing she had not done publicly in five years. Death in the house was bad enough in itself. "Damn the luck!" she had moaned, running where Zebby's squalls announced the tragedy. For, staring at the marred lips, shaking the limp body, she had known what looks, what cries would come behind her, what dark curse for days would fret The Mansion. And here was no whisper persisting through the town; here was a shout from the housetops. Only once before had a girl of Thelma's seen fit to quit the imperial palace by suicide. May was a Judas among the fortunate disciples, betraying her mistress into the hands of her enemies.

Nevertheless, she saw to May's funeral. To do so was part of the code of her profession—and, Thelma reflected, good policy, the girls feeling so blue and all. So she had paid for the laying away of this flesh which had served her, and even attended the obsequies by which it was given back to the dust.

That was Saturday. In the early afternoon, with Lilyan, Thelma attended the baseball game, her one habit uncalculating of profit to herself. When the sun glinted red on the big bull above the right-field fence and Wild Bill Banks cinched the double-header for the Moccasins with his fourteenth strikeout, she was in a box directly behind home plate. She stood up, clapping her hands, as torrents of men converged across the diamond. "Oh, you Bill!" shrilled Thelma. Bow legs were caught up on the shoulders of the mob. Money pelted. "Oh, you Bill!" shrieked Thelma again. For a moment she was a child.

Both women began buttoning their gloves. They wore white gloves and white veils despite the heat of the day, and as they moved toward the exit, their faces took on starched, buttoned expressions. This air of disdain, their conversation, clothes were no different from those of any two ladies at a ball game, yet something—a bristling, a challenge—seemed to freight them with an outlaw quality that compelled glances.

"Shove along, Lil," complained Thelma. "I'm hot as hell."

They went by a stair which took them beneath the grandstand. In privileged space stood a limousine with a mulatto boy at the wheel, and into this the two stepped and went spinning through the gates and through the throngs struggling around the trolley cars, and so out an avenue which grew broader and its residences more and more imposing. This was Green Hills.

Usually, to emerge from her lair and whisk unrecognized among these lawns and hedges and stately homes, gave Thelma pleasure more sensual than any physical contact. The only other Pierce-Arrow in town was owned by old Mrs. Van Terhune. Thelma knew the Van Terhune heir well. She was sure the populace frequently mistook her for his mother, and the thought gratified her. But today her observing eyes were bitter. Green Hills no longer was a promised land; it was the citadel of a world turned hostile, and in every granite wall she saw power before which she was helpless, in every sunlit window the flash of a destroying bayonet.

The limousine dropped grandeur behind for a section of poorer houses, some no better than cabins and others gimcrack bungalows, and soon these gave way to field and woodland and patches of corn and truck gardens. Dust from the road painted the edges gold and lay on the flags of corn and on the rows of vegetables. Only deep in the woods—and perhaps dust was there, too—did anything seem not dry and burned. But suddenly, not far ahead, rose above the highway a slope of green on which white dots became, as they neared them, white slabs hugging the turf and white monuments pinnacling above it, with a white wall circling to the sky the green slope it embraced. Springing out of the scarred lands, this Eden was so unexpected, so cool that it would have impressed even without the realization that there were the dead.

Thelma and Lilyan left the limousine outside the gate, though there was no rule against cars entering the cemetery. They had imagined there must be, for somehow all sound seemed indecorous here. They walked very precisely along a white path among the graves, and the hush closed around them so that the crunch, crunch of their heels in the gravel was loud and harsh. The old man at the gate had directed them. He said that the Smith funeral party—May Smith they had called her in The Mansion and as May Smith she would be buried—had but just gone in and doubtless was at the grave, which, he informed them with some pride, he had dug that morning in the lot over the crest of the hill beyond the more pretentious memorials. The walk was long and it was still hot, though the sun was down. The ribbons of Thelma's underwear slipped on her shoulders but though her fingers itched to adjust them, she pressed her nails into her palms and let the straps rub while the marble watchers judged her as she crunched past. So, coming out from a grove of crêpe myrtle, she saw in a dip a hearse drawn up to one side of the road and behind it a liveryman's hack. The only persons in sight were three men. One in black stood waiting. Two others stooped where a heap of earth caught the afterglow and shone like gold.

The casket had been lowered into the grave by the time Thelma and Lilyan drew close. They paused at what seemed a proper place, watching the two men tug at the heavy straps and trying not to appear interested. The two men walked away a little distance, wiping their faces, and the younger stumbled and turned a hot red, and Thelma knew he tripped because he had been covertly studying them, and that he blushed because he was ashamed. The preacher, who had bowed at their approach, opened a little book and, after a quick glance, began to speak.

There had been funerals in Thelma's childhood, for death was the superlative event in Catamount and whole families travelled miles for the buryings of no matter how distant kin. But she had slept in the wagon or played with the other children or, even when she fidgeted through endless prayers, scarcely known which cousin or aunt she fidgeted for. Death was a bore then and death still vexed rather than depressed her. May's funeral, she had been thinking that morning, wasn't *her* funeral; why bother? Yet here she was, and absorbed no more by foes and calamities and intrigues—worrying over the hundred extra the lieutenant was demanding, suspecting that the undertaker might substitute a cheaper coffin for the one she had picked—but in dread only that she would make some sound, a sneeze, a regurgitation, that would shatter the solemn quiet all around her.

"Man that is born of woman hath but a short time to live and is full of misery. He cometh up, and is cut down, like a flower; he fleeth as it were a shadow, and never continueth in one stay."

The words tinkled thinly in the still, echoless air, and though they carried to Thelma no keen sense, no deep meaning, they fell fatefully on the ear. She wished that she had not come.

"O, Lord God most holy, O Lord most mighty, O holy and most merciful Saviour, deliver us not into the bitter pains of eternal death."

The bitter pains of eternal death. It was so green and lovely here with things growing and a smell of earth in the air. The liveryman's horse stamped and you knew that if you went over and stroked him, the heat of the sun would be in his sides, and the odour of horse and leather would be rankly pleasant. Even the hole they had dug for May did not seem bitter, painful, dark. May would lie there wrapped in warmth and fragrance.

The minister bent. Earth clasped his fingers to the knuckles.

"Forasmuch as it hath pleased Almighty God, in his wise providence, to take out of this world the soul of our deceased sister, we therefore commit her body—ashes to ashes, dust to dust—"

The clods fell—thump—thump—and all the ordered thoughts in Thelma's head fell with them, the quiet, the brightness, the warmth and fragrance, they split into a glare, then a blackness, crashing, crashing, black, black, and voices jeering—"Ashes to ashes, dust to dust, if the women don't get you—if the women don't get you—get, get, get you—" She grabbed at Lilyan's sleeve.

"But, dearie—You can't!"

The hoarse whisper gave the minister pause. He looked up to see his audience going away from there, and his mouth opened in amazement. But, being a young man and even then wondering what he would say to those two when the service was over, he was not unrelieved. The other two, the undertaker's assistants, were some way off, absorbed in pitching pebbles at a tombstone. So he finished reading the beautiful words alone, thinking how beautiful they were and that it was a little sad there was none to hear them save himself and the liveryman's horse and—perhaps?—the soul of May Smith.

Lilyan had jerked her arm free. She stalked with head in air, feeling never so humiliated in her life. Even one's landlady—"My dear, I was never so humiliated in my life! Right in the middle she lit out without so much as a 'Beg your pardon!' It was—humiliating!"

And the clods still thumped, thumped into the dark. The strangling dark, to bury you forever in the dark! They lay on her breast, heavy, heavier. And no good to struggle, no good to pant and scratch! Oh, she could not die! She could not die!

The limousine cuddled her reassuringly.

"Home, Willie," she said, and sat up uxoriously to the rush of air.

Twilight was long past when the car escaped from the heavy downtown traffic and darted at last across Hamilton Viaduct. Night rose from the underpass like a great, swallowing mouth, but it was night Thelma knew as she knew her own face, lurid, hot, fetid, noisome—alive. Night with a jangle and a shriek in it. "Ashes to ashes, dust to dust"—umpa, umpa—"if the women don't get you, well, the cocaine must!" She smiled. Saturday night on Kelso Street. ...

Sweat-pale faces danced in the gloom outside her car window. The horn was going it. There—Willie had almost hit somebody. Damn fool! A woman, too. Must be drunk. But the car was slowing. Why, this was The Mansion! And a mob outside. What the devil? Stung with exasperation and foreboding, she flung open the door. The din of brass and drums was frightful, but the voices shouted clear above it.

Whiter than snow! Whi-ter than snow!
Wash me and I will be whiter than snow!

Standing on the steps of the limousine, Thelma screamed like a maniac. But the cloaked shapes paid no attention. She might as well have been singing with them.

CHAPTER SIX
CRUSADE (continued)

THE ALARM CLOCK rang at eleven this Saturday morning, but Curtis Rowlett, after cutting it off, did not get up until five minutes past twelve. His hang-over made the sunshine blinding. Sitting on the edge of the bed in the shirt and underdrawers he had slept in, he tried to remember drearily all that had happened. The bunch at Charlie Harper's; a lot of beer and then, like a fool, whisky on top of it; out to Fred Gaston's place, everybody pretty drunk—with a shock it came to him that he had lost money in the crap game. A lor of money. "Shoot the piece?"—"You're faded"—somebody blubbering, "I've lost it all! I've lost my money! Damn you, you got my money!"—and somebody else telling him to shut up—"You're drunk, Curtis." God—what a fool! To shoot craps that way ... drunk. ...

His trousers lay on the floor. He put them on, brushing weakly at the lint, and ran through the pockets. Not a cent. And pay-day was yesterday—he'd have to borrow again. While he donned the same shirt he had worn the day before, turning the cuffs, he frowned over prospects. A dollar here, two dollars there—Jesus! it was rotten to have to bum these grudged driblets. If he had a real salary; if he could work a regular loan, say a hundred dollars; maybe if he tried that Benefactor Plan, got somebody to go on his note—a damn shame not to have money! Here he was his own man, in his own place since he told his family where to get off, a fellow with talent, a fellow with powerful friends, a *newspaperman*— shucks, if he had money, he could live like a prince!

Like a prince. ... He fumbled around the narrow little room, hunting for a cigarette, and finally found a butt under the bed near the slop jar. Into a basin he poured water from a pitcher, soused his head, combed back the hair to a dripping gloss, and went out to breakfast at the Greek's, dragging hard on his pinch of tobacco. He looked clean.

Only in the light of future events—some of them occurring years afterward—did the movements of Curtis Rowlett that day take on interest to those who knew him. It was recalled by the city editor of the Star-Register that Rowlett reported by telephone from police headquarters at one o'clock and that at two he was in the office, where he wrote several items of arrests and court news and borrowed a dollar from Buck Nivens, a copy reader. Nivens remembered perfectly, for the dollar was never returned.

Others had vaguer but more salient recollections.

A patrolman, one Bob Fane, was approached by Curtis at the corner of Faith and Magnolia Streets, south of Bucktown, early Saturday afternoon.

"Say, Bob," said Curtis, "there's a nigger over in the next block you ought to run in."

"What for?"

"Con game. He's sellin' stuff without a license—some sort of rattlesnake oil or somethin'."

"Oh, what the hell? Niggers—"

"I know. But he hasn't got a license. And this is a good story. You know him—old Frog Bell. He's been pinched before. One time he was sellin' tickets to heaven—remember? He's always up to some phony stuff."

The patrolman was not averse to his name in the paper where his wife and neighbours would see it. He knew Rowlett would "take care of him." He arrested Frog Bell.

Another who never forgot Curtis was the turnkey at the city prison. About four o'clock the reporter talked for some time to an old Negro brought in on a minor charge. The turnkey remembered that the old Negro had scratched something on a piece of paper, and that Rowlett stuck this in his pocket. "What's that?" the turnkey had asked, for he considered nobody above suspicion.

"Just a note to his lawyer. He's a nigger that used to work for me and I promised to help him out. What's this stuff, Steve?"

Curtis was leaning on the turnkey's desk, poking among the claptrap frisked from prisoners. His fingers lingered on a number of small green bottles.

"That? Came off the nigger you was talkin' to. Some sort of nigger dope. You better keep your mitts outen them things, young feller."

"Oh, all right, Steve!"

Curtis slapped the turnkey on the back so that the man capsized head down.

"You durn little squirt!" he choked.

But Curtis slipped out of reach and ran from the jail, laughing.

Afterward the turnkey had a notion that one of the little bottles was missing. He could not be sure. But the suspicion nourished the wrath he already treasured for that slap. The durn little squirt. ...

Trivial incidents, but the day was to come when they would be part of the astonishing legend of Curtis Rowlett, his obscurity, his foxiness and his rise. For the turnkey grumbled his resentment, and Patrolman Fane talked, and these matters came to the ears of other reporters on the Star-Register in their wonder over Curtis Rowlett's mysterious disappearance, so that when they became old- timers and yarned on Saturday nights, the yarn they told with keenest envy was the yarn of the police reporter who saw his luck and grabbed it. According to their tale, he discovered in his prowlings a conjure man with a liquid of strange properties, and the conjure man he cleverly caused to be arrested, and this fellow, by shrewd means, he persuaded to sign away all rights to his nostrum, the secret of which the reporter procured by juggling from under the nose of the police a bottle which he took to a chemist. What followed everyone knows.

This was the tale, and with due allowance for some glorification of Curtis Rowlett, it was accurate as far as it went. Only it did not go as far as the door to The Mansion.

Thence Curtis hurried from Frog Bell, and asked for Thelma, and was put out to learn that she was absent at May's funeral. He sat for a while with Carmen, drinking a bottle of beer, and then strolled toward the police station, clasping the vial in his pocket and wondering whether he could reach Thelma's side before her Saturday night rush began.

It must, he thought, be getting on toward seven o'clock. Dusk brought no cool hand on that part of the city, choked with saloons and pawnshops and auction houses and penny arcades. Suddenly the arclights flared and night, instead of space and stars, was a funnel pressing hot around the street. In the funnel churned an ant-heap ninety per cent black, and noise and stench hung above it as if the funnel's sides refused them escape into the dark. A bell inside an auction house began to ring, its piercing drill as insistent as a riveting machine's. It would ring that way without let-up until midnight.

Curtis, stopping on a corner, was very undecided. If he continued to the police station, he must get in touch with the office. If he got in touch with the office, he must work. And his present fancy bounded far ahead of mere work. If he could see Thelma—only a few minutes—

Above the racket of the street a drum throbbed—rumbumbum, a rum-bum-bum—and the beat, far off at first, drew closer so that Curtis swung around and strained his eyes through the glare and the dark and the jostling crowds. Others were peering too. Negroes ran past him, shouting, "At's a ban', boy! Yes, suh! Yes, suh!" and, indeed, to the rum-bum of the drum joined the high whine of a fife, a bugle blew, and there rose an undertone of voices cheering or singing. It was certainly a parade. He could detect a moving mass slashed with glimpses of white and a lofty banner, and then, as the phalanx debouched into the street lamp's radius, he saw that these were neither minstrels nor militia nor Knights of Pythias, but such a parade as Peachburg had not witnessed in all its patriotic and fraternal history.

A ragtag of Negro urchins spilled before, filling the street to the curbs, for those who could not march next the drummer strove for that place. They wriggled and fought, yet they all kept step and most of. them kept time, too, with a "Bam!—Bam! Bamity! Bamity!—Bam!" crooned to the drum's boom. After the band a gap of about twenty yards and in the middle of it, striding alone, a standard-bearer. It was not, after all, a flag that he bore, but a sheet tacked to a cross-pole, and the flutter of it was not so confusing but that all could recognize the splash of black and red as a gorilla with a naked woman tucked under his arm. The copy did not do justice to the model—the gorilla seemed mild and somewhat tired—but the lettering made up what he lacked in violence. "Beast!—Red Light!—Purity!" Curtis recognized the standard- bearer as Jethro Harris.

"On-ward, Christian so-el-jers!" sang the women. There were not a hundred of them, but bursting out of the lurid shadow in their white hoods and long white capes, chanting their war cry,

they seemed a thousand. "Forward into ba-a-t-ul!" they sang—
how they sang! The torrent of darkies swept on and over Curtis,
and he went with them.

Police headquarters was a lonely place early in the evening.
Court was long over, lawyers and witnesses and hangers-on were
vanished, the watch had been changed at six, and in the call-
room two motorcycle policemen gossiped idly with the sergeant.
Not for several hours would the round-up of Saturday night
brawlers start lurching through the porticoes where now shreds
of paper flapped unremarked. But, as Jethro and his cohorts
advanced like a hurricane out of the torpid night, they brought
tumult with them. Lights flashed in windows, heads stuck out,
porches suddenly came alive with uniforms, and over stairs and
buttresses the crowd billowed.

"Halt!" shouted Jethro.

Curtis swore at the Negroes who blocked his way. He clawed
for entrance, a chance to telephone the office. For a crisis was in
the making, and he, who knew so little yet so much, had felt the
thrill of it from the moment Jethro's Philatheas surged singing in
the tread of the brass band.

"For-ward into battle, see His banners go!"

He broke through tatters that resisted and struck, and
plunged free across a court. Home ground. A stairway—and he
took it running. His hand went to his pocket—the vial was safe.
Up—a left turn—and he was on the second floor. The next room
was the Chief's. He could telephone there.

As he started along the empty corridor, the hullabaloo outside cut loose again. Jethro had ended an exhortation and they
were singing once more, "There Is a Fountain Filled with Blood,"
one woman's falsetto curdling high above the others and the
drum going like a voodoo queen's. Curtis, with another step,
halted as though a gun had been levelled at him.

For through the open door, looking directly into the austere room with its desk and files and atrocious oils of dead police heroes, he beheld its lone occupant in an attitude as alien to his office as a game of croquet. Luke Palmer was on his knees in the centre of the matting, his hat off and his weather-beaten face lifted and his eyes shut tight, and there was no doubt whatever that Luke Palmer was praying.

For a minute or more, while the man's lips moved and in the hard light even the veins of his eyelids stood out clear, Curtis watched, too astounded to flex a muscle. Then another savage boom welled through the windows, and to the watcher in a flash came the events of months with all their threats and shadings—the reform election, the Chief's wife and church affiliations, his gambling raids and summary dismissal of subordinates, the whole pattern of city politics with its unrest and mutterings and fears and Jethro's hammer pounding in the middle of it, pounding now in his very ears—and Curtis knew the hour had struck.

Fifteen minutes later, as horses were being backed between the shafts of patrol wagons and four lines of bluecoats clicked to attention before a puzzled captain of detectives, the sidewalks were deserted. Crusaders and camp-followers had swept on to the pit of evil, and the squad that followed, wheeling from the sooty porticoes toward the distant clap of riot, moved with no accompaniment but the thud of their own feet. At their head stumped Luke Palmer, ungracefully but resolved, as Gideon may have marched at the head of his ten to cast down the altar of Baal.

Curtis was at the door of The Mansion before Jethro was on the move again, he was in the parlour arguing frantically with Carmen as the brass band swung into Kelso Street, and he was out, one of the mob, when Thelma's limousine foundered among the shoals of Philatheas. The district, by then, roared. Out of the houses tumbled the sober and the drunken to swell the whooping, laughing circus, the painted women jeered or stared bewildered, the Philatheas sang, the band played, and the smoky roof of the viaduct flung back the clamour.

"Thelma!" he shouted. "Thelma!" But she was marooned on the limousine steps, shrieking her unheard curses on the heads of the godly. He got to her at the price of torn buttons, tugged her down, urged her through the scuffle, at last hustled her into the Mansion, was actually pushing her up the grand staircase before she broke away and demanded, in the name of hell and Moses, what he meant.

He was panting and dishevelled, yet even then his hand felt for the vial in his pocket.

"It's a raid. ... Not that crazy bunch out there. ... The cops! They're comin' sure as God made little apples. You wanta get out quick!"

She snarled, at that instant not a whit removed from the first tigress. All the cops in Peachburg weren't going to keep Thelma LaMont from doing combat with a skunk who had publicly branded her and now impudently sang hymns on her doorstep.

"To hell with the cops!"

"For God's sake, Thelma, do you wanta go to jail? They'll run you in sure. They'll close your house and take all you got. I tell you I saw Luke Palmer, and he means business. This ain't no little bitsy raid—this is the works!"

All you got. ... They'd done it before, hadn't they? All the pretties, all the fascinating pretties. Nothing left but a few dollars—such a few beside the present bank balance of Thelma LaMont and the present cashroll in the safe in Thelma LaMont's bedroom. What was to stop them? The law? She knew a trick or two about the law. But they *were* the law. And Charlie Harper had said what he said of Kelso Street and Luke Palmer's right to crack down whenever he was a mind to.

"Curtis, if you're stringing me—"

"For God's sake, hurry!"

She turned and galloped up the stairs.

Her own room snug around her, she hesitated. The rose lamp shed security on rugs and drapes and pictures, and the walls reached out to hold her fast. Her vanity dresser—she could not take that with her, nor the chaise- longue, nor the lace pillow, nor the etching of Notre Dame she had always thought was Westminster Abbey. The dresses in her closet—by God, she'd stay and fight! She couldn't run away and leave the dresses! Glass crashed below. It was only a stone shied by a roisterer, but at the muffled tinkle Thelma sprang to the safe, jerked the handles and began to sweep the contents into a travelling bag. As she worked, her mind raced—after all, no harm getting out—she'd come back, she'd sue if they touched a single camisole—and that jewel box, and the drawer full of trinkets, and the cameo pin— holy heaven! where was the pin? She ran crazily from dresser to safe. Damn! she had it on all the time! One hand stripped a shelf of its load of underwear. She tore a fur from a hook and a coat off its hanger. The bag brimmed, but she stuffed it down, throwing in the green-heeled slippers. If the strap broke!—heaving and sweating, the coat on one arm and the bag all but pulling the other from its socket, she gave a last look. Her free hand plucked the big perfume bottle from the dresser. ...

"Good Lord!" groaned Curtis. But he took the bag.

From the canopied hall of The Mansion, through the open door, the figures of the professor and the girls chopped black splotches against the street's glare. And now these wavered, and up the steps into the path of light advanced a head above brawny shoulders.

"Come on!" urged Curtis, for he believed the police were upon them.

But the voice that rolled across the threshold, crying the names of Thelma LaMont and God, was not the voice of Luke Palmer nor any of his men.

Not for a mere serenade had Jethro planned all the week, not for a skyrocket that should fizzle after one pop. To march on Sodom was splendid, to exhort the Chief in passing an inspiration, but Jethro's scheme had never contemplated stopping there. The Lord was with him, the Lord demanded penitents, and for the Lord he would nail the fattest penitent of the lot, though he personally walked into hell and took a good, long look.

"Thelma LaMont, come out!"

It was Jethro's big moment—Ethan Allen demanding Ticonderoga in the name of the Great Jehovah and the Continental Congress. Yet, though there are 864 pages in the report of the Christ and Purity League on the crusade against the red light in Peachburg, you will find mentioned nowhere the details of its most stirring encounter. The fact is a little pathetic, since it would seem to indicate that Jethro never recognized his arch-enemy as she cantered into the grand finale he had arranged.

What happened was this: As Curtis, charging ahead with the bag, dodged to one side, and Thelma, at his heels, found her exit blocked by a large man shouting gibberish, her irritation boiled over. Her right arm swung. It would be too much to wonder whether recognition was hers; whether, in that second face to face, memory of a backwoods sorcerer came yelling down the years to quicken her stroke. The blackest strumpet, they say, never forgets the circumstances of her first fall, but Thelma probably was quite unaware that she had winged a preacher. Jethro went down with a slow sag, fifty dollars' worth of attar of roses immersing him.

At the head of the street, gongs clanged wildly where men and women scattered before the plunging horses. Curtis jammed his salvage through the limousine door, tossed the bag on top of her and jumped to the running board beside the scared chauffeur.

"Beat it!" he shouted. The motor roared.

A typhoon seemed to smite him. Blindly he kicked out at this fury of robes and claws, grabbed an arm, held off the woman whose contorted face bit up at him.

"She hit him! She hit him! She hit him!"

Curtis put the heel of his palm into the Philathea's mouth as a blue shoulder lunged between them.

"What the hell—"

"She hit him!"

"Don't you believe it, officer, the God damn whore! She's drunk. This is Bob Van Terhune's car and that's Bob in the back. You don't want to arrest *him,* do you?"

And so, as the uplift came to Kelso Street, Thelma LaMont left it—in one of the only two Pierce-Arrows in Peachburg.

CHAPTER SEVEN
WHITEINE

I T WAS MAY, 1917, seven years after the cleansing of Peachburg. On the Caneyville road two women met, one tall and skinny and yellow, the other like a chunk of new tar in the sun. As they passed, the tall one said something. The other turned and shook her fist. "Go 'long, no 'count high yaller!" she shouted. "Go 'long, no 'count high yaller!" And for some time, trudging on alone in the hot red dust, she mumbled to herself.

At the store she bought a dime's worth of bacon and half a peck of meal. While the storekeeper made change out of money kept in a crocus sack, she glowered at a sign above the counter. It was doubtful if she could read, but perhaps she had seen such a sign before.

"You got de stuff in de sign?" she asked, and the storekeeper nodded. He showed her a small bottle.

"How much?"

"Fo' bits," said the storekeeper.

"Fo' bits?" repeated the Negro. "Fo' bits?—Lawd Gawd, white man!" And she went out, mumbling.

A man lounging in the store laughed.

"Don't you worry, Mr. Potts," he said. "She'll be back!"

"Mebbe," said the storekeeper.

Not a quarter of a mile along the Caneyville road the trudging, black Negro was overtaken by a Ford. It stopped, and the man who had been in the store leaned out.

"How far to Caneyville, auntie?"

" 'Bout five mile."

"You want some of that stuff you asked about in the store, auntie?"

She yawed her eyes suspiciously.

"Whut you talkin' 'bout, white man?"

Then she perceived that he held up a bottle and that the side of the Ford was decorated with letters similar to those in the sign at Potts's store. He was an agent—she had seen agents before.

"How much?"

"Won't cost you a cent, auntie. You just gimme a testimonial."

"Testi—whut?"

"You just gimme a testimonial, auntie. Here—it says you tried it and it done you good. You just write your name here, or make your mark, and it just says it done you good and we can print your picture in the paper. That's all—and you git the bottle for nothin'."

"Whar'bouts you gwiner git my picture? How I'se gwiner know it done me good if I ain't tried it yit?"

"Don't you worry 'bout no picture. And how you gonna try it if you don't gimme the testimonial first?"

Morosely she eyed him, but at last allowed him to hand her the bottle and to write down her name and R.F.D. address and to guide her fingers to the spot where she scratched an "X."

"Kain't see to write widout mah glasses," she apologized.

The Ford racketed away.

In Caneyville, at the Palmetto Hotel, the man spent an hour over long, formlike sheets. These he stuffed into an envelope, ready addressed to Complexion Refineries, Inc., and this envelope was on the six o'clock train for Corinth, the state capital.

The headquarters of Complexion Refineries, Inc., occupied an entire wing on the eleventh floor of the Nickajack Building, referred to locally as a skyscraper. They consisted of two rooms, each as big as a tennis court, and opening off them several smaller rooms on the glass doors of which glittered "Private," "Vice-President," "Auditor" and other identifications. By nine in the morning the two big rooms were filled with workers. Most of these were girls, some typing, others clipping and filing, one running a noisy machine for automatic addressing. In a corner of one room, four coatless men smoked and occasionally talked.

A boy brought the mail for Complexion Refineries, Inc., from the post office three times a day. He dumped the heavy sack on the desk of Mr. Rowlett, the Vice- President. Here Mr. Rowlett's secretary sorted it and the boy distributed all but the "factory mail." The "testimonial mail" went to the four men in the corner. Mr. Meeker, the head copy man, looked it over. Some he filed and some he parcelled between his two assistants. The fourth man sat at a drawing-board. He had pen, ink and an air-brush. He was an expert "retoucher."

"This isn't bad," said Mr. Mecker to the youngest assistant. "Amanda Cobb—good name—R.F.D. Catamount—wherever the hell that is—'One bottle of your product'—and so on. See if you can't bull that along for a thousand words, son. Give it class—'well-known social leader, extreme brunette type, humiliated for years by her complexion problem, envied fairer friends'—ring in something about hair, too—but make it plausible, give it dignity. You gotta get punch and dignity. These shines are sensitive as hell. Study those ads in 'Vogue' and 'Vanity Fair.' Punch, Authority, Snob Appeal—that's the ticket."

Mr. Mecker's eyes galloped over Amanda Cobb's tribute.

"No picture, but description says about fifty, very black, a 'lippy' nigger. Whatever the hell that means. Scar on left cheek. … Harrison, get a good pic out of the morgue. Have a couple of veloxes made—we'll do a 'Before and After.' Put the scar in the first one. Evening dress and a necklace in Number Two. And for glory's sake, go heavy on the white! By the time some of these country papers get ink on a cut, it looks like the queen of clubs."

The man at the drawing-board got up and began to rumple through the contents of a steel cabinet. It contained the relics of a photographer gone bankrupt in Chicago's black belt.

"Let me see her, will you, Harrison?" said the youngest assistant. Somehow it helped him to look upon his subjects, even though he knew they were phony. They soothed the feeling of utter preposterousness that was apt to nag him when he attacked the typewriter.

Neal Carver, the youngest assistant, had occupied that position only a few weeks. He had not yet been able to shake off the delusion that he was one of a company of players in some burlesque show. It was absurd to believe that money—hundreds of thousands, they said—was being made by this tomfoolery. Absurd to think that anyone believed what he wrote. Absurd to trot out these etiolated puppets and introduce them as "Mr. This" and "Mrs. That" when they were only a scrabble of Negroes and half the time not even genuine. But he must learn, he must make good. Complexion Refineries had taken him from a piddling newspaper job and jumped him to a salary of fifty dollars a week. So he wrote, earnestly:

SOUTHERN SOCIETY MATRON'S
VERY ASTONISHING EXPERIENCE

The wizardly Mr. Meeker, who could conjure such heads as "I LAUGH AT JIM CROW LAWS SINCE TRYING WHITEINE," probably would change this one. But Carver was eager. With the photograph of a marcelled octoroon propped before him, he proceeded.

"For years my complexion was my cross," writes Mrs. Amanda Cobb, prominent Southern society matron. "I was a deep brunette. My skin was an ugly dark brown and my hair kinked in spite of all efforts to wave it. Often I envied my fairer friends their ivory skin and long, straight, lovely tresses. I wished that I, too, had a complexion men admire and women envy. I wished that I might experience the benefits they enjoyed and escape the annoyances which are so frequently the penalty of dark, ugly, shiny features. I asked myself why, with all the progress made by science and invention, something had not been done to help dark skin and kinky hair? Then, one day, a Chicago society lady famous for her milky complexion revealed her secret to me. 'Why,' she said, 'do you not use WHITEINE?' I told her I had never heard of it. Then she explained to me that expert chemists, working in government laboratories, had discovered a formula which private capital had successfully converted into a boon to our Race—"

The youngest assistant paused, scratched out "boon" and substituted "blessing." Mr. Meeker had accused him of being literary. He read over what he had written. So far so good—no offensive words like "black" or "Negro," but "brunette" and "Race" (always capitalized); the impression that these were high-toned people; a reference (not too crude) to the "penalties" of being black; then Authority, the expert chemists working in government laboratories. "But won't the government object to that?" he had asked Mr. Meeker the first time he wrote the phrase. "To what?" Mr. Mecker had retorted. "Son, there never was a formula that didn't go back somewhere to some government's laboratories. And if private capital *converts* it, you're safe. Look it up in Webster—'Convert, to change into another state, form or substance.' Well, the formula for Whiteine may originally have been the formula for pigs' knuckles—I dunno—Rowlett dug it up somewhere—but we took it and we converted it and we're grateful to the government and so are the shines grateful. Whatever else you write, remember always to put that into every piece of copy."

So the youngest assistant learned never to leave out Authority. But he still wondered, sometimes, just what it was the government chemists had discovered and how private capital had converted it into the blessing. Private capital—whose?

Nobody in Corinth seemed to know much about the powers behind Complexion Refineries, Inc. Nobody had ever heard of it until a few years before, when those funny advertisements began to appear. The Corinth papers refused to take them; they were a majestic press devoted to the new credo of "Truth in Advertising." But in the country weeklies, in the Corinth Negro daily, in all the stores in the Negro quarter, one saw "Whiteine" advertised. Carver and the other reporters used to laugh over them—"Pullman Porter Gets Life-Long Wish," "How I Won My Husband," "They Teased Me About My Colour." And then, one day, Mr. Meeker, who used to work on the Blade, came into the office and asked him to have a Coca-Cola and in the soda fountain downstairs made his proposition.

"If you want big money, you got to get where the big money is," Mr. Meeker had said.

Young Carver didn't want big money; he wanted to write a play. But he knew he could never write a play until he made enough money to go to New York and live in Greenwich Village, where he would have the time and the proper atmosphere in which to write. So he took the job where the big money was. His family hadn't exactly approved—a Carver had been governor of that state once, and it seemed grisly for a Carver to be working for a complexion company or even writing a play—but his mother, who hadn't known what a reporter was when Neal went to work for the Blade, protested but feebly. They were very poor and, with Berenice pining to go to Miss Meredith's Seminary, somebody in the family had to make money.

"Who owns this company, Neal?" she had asked.

"Some Northern people, I think."

He honestly hadn't known. And he still didn't know. Over at the Blade they said a fellow named Curtis Rowlett owned it and that this Rowlett had been a newspaper man himself once and was a humdinger. A regular hustler. He had seen Rowlett, and he was startled to discover that Rowlett didn't look much older than he was.

He watched Rowlett come and go through the office in his swell suits and his silk shirts and a cigar always in his mouth, and he wondered how it would feel to have your own car and be as rich as blazes. Gosh! Why didn't a fellow like that cut loose and write a play if he'd been a newspaper man himself once? He said to Mr. Meeker, "Rowlett owns this company, doesn't he?"—"He's got stock in it," said Mr. Meeker.—"I guess he's pretty smart fellow," commented Carver.—"In a pig's eye," said Mr. Meeker. But Carver noticed that Mr. Meeker jumped fast enough when he was wanted in the Vice-President's office.

Rowlett was in there now with some out-of-town fellow. Mr. Mecker had gone downstairs with Harrison and Blake for a Coca-Cola, and the youngest assistant was temporarily alone. "A blessing to our Race," he read again. The door to the outer office opened and closed, and a voice quietly said:

"Young man, will you go in there and tell Mr. Rowlett I want him?"

Carver had never seen before the lady who thus addressed him. She was, to his eyes, not "young" yet certainly not "old"—that is to say, she was not young in the budding, rippling way most of the girls he knew were young, nor was she anywhere near the age of his mother, whom he thought of as "old" at forty-eight. This lady's smooth, rose cheeks might have belonged to any schoolgirl, her eyes were bright pale blue, and her figure was lithe where she bent a little toward him. Yet she commanded more than mere admiration. Perhaps it was the unswerving intentness of her gaze, perhaps it was the clothes she wore—they struck even young Carver as singularly smart, though they were simply tailored and she showed no jewels save a cameo at her throat—or perhaps it was her voice, which was low but with a quality that immediately unsettled him. He got up and bowed, wondering who delivered such abrupt orders.

"I think Mr. Rowlett's engaged."

"Indeed? Just the same—tell him to come here, please. And come alone."

"Yes, ma'am." Carver was amazed at his own surrender. "Shall I give any name?"

The lady stared. For a moment, he feared she was going to be quite angry. But suddenly, after a scrutiny that unsettled him more than ever, she smiled.

"I am Mrs. Potter."

"Yes, ma'am," repeated Carver, and went to do her bidding.

The Vice-President was thrust back in an easy-chair with his feet on his desk. The out-of-town fellow balanced on a chair opposite, and there was a bottle between them. The Vice-President frowned at Carver, but as soon as the message was delivered, he acted with alacrity. There was even, thought Carver, an expression of panic on his face as his feet came down and his body came up.

"Wait a minute, Charlie," said the Vice-President.

They were talking by the window, the lady and the Vice-President, when Carver reached his desk again, and though he could hear nothing but a low rumble, he had the feeling one often has that the lady was giving the Vice-President what-for.

Mrs. Potter left after a moment and Mr. Rowlett returned to his office. Pretty soon the other fellow left.

"Anybody want me?" asked Mr. Meeker, when he came in with Blake and Harrison.

"No," said Carver. "There was a lady, but she came to see Mr. Rowlett."

"Not Mrs. Potter?"

"Yes—that's who it was."

Mr. Mecker groaned. "Oh, my good glory! now we're in for more hell."

Mr. Meeker got busy at his desk; Carver studied the sheet of paper in his typewriter. But his mind wandered from government laboratories. A faint odour of violets lingered in the air. It disturbed him, not sentimentally, but because it brought back Mrs. Potter's scrutinizing eyes and his own jumpy feeling which the Vice-President had seemed to share.

"Say, Mr. Meeker," he asked at last, "who is Mrs. Potter?"

"Son, Mrs. Potter is Complexion Refineries, Inc.—all of it. She keeps books on *every* carload of Whiteine sold between here and Seattle and if you're a wise laddie, you won't forget to say 'Yes, ma'am' and 'No, ma'am' any time she looks your way."

Carver sincerely hoped Mrs. Potter would not again look his way. There were many things about this business he had yet to understand, and Mrs. Potter's look was one of them.

" 'Successfully converted into a blessing to our Race,' " he murmured, and fastened his gaze wistfully on the photograph that was soon to be Mrs. Amanda Cobb.

What Mrs. Potter had said to the Vice-President was this:

"Look here, Curtis, is that Charlie Harper in there?"

"Why—yes, it is Charlie."

Mrs. Potter's face did something queer to itself. It lost its smoothly tailored look—it lumped into a sort of fist.

"I thought so. I saw you come in the building together. What's he doing here?"

"Why, he's not doing anything. I just met him—just happened to run into him. He hollered at me. I couldn't pass him up, could I? I asked him to come up a minute."

The fist of Mrs. Potter's face clenched.

"Had to show off, didn't you? The millionaire kid! Well, I've stood this for the last time, Curtis. I've told you repeatedly I won't have any of that Peachburg trash around. If I thought you were playing me tricks—"

"Aw, cut it, Thelma! I told you how it was—honest."

The Vice-President's arm stung to a pinching grip.

"Don't ever use that name!" whispered Mrs. Potter, violently. She swung her eyes toward the youngest assistant hunched over his typewriter. Then her face sprung smooth as though someone had touched a button.

Mrs. Potter put on her gloves.

"By the way, who is that young man?" she inquired. "I haven't seen him before."

"Oh, he's nobody. A new assistant Mecker's got. His name's Carver. He was on the Blade. Listen, Genevieve, you know I'm on the level with you."

"Sure, I know. You get Harper out of here and get him quick."

The fist flashed and disappeared on its hidden springs. Mrs. Potter passed out through the two big rooms. Her heels clicked dainty clicks. Now and then, as a girl lifted her head, Mrs. Potter smiled charmingly.

The Vice-President was back in his office, telling Charlie Harper he was sorry but he had "a conference." The visitor rose. It did beat all, that good-for-nothin' Curtis Rowlett struttin' around like a durn duke, and made it all turnin' black niggers white.

After the departure, the Vice-President took the bottle and glasses from the table, placed them in a desk drawer and was about to lock it, when some powerful emotion overcame him. His lips moved as though words spouted from their corners, he took out the bottle and a glass again, poured, and tossed off his drink with a gulp. Then he glared across the table.

"I'll see who I durn please!" said the Vice-President to the empty room.

CHAPTER EIGHT
RICH MRS. POTTER

I T WAS characteristic of Mrs. Potter that she thought no more of the conversation with Curtis Rowlett from the instant she tapped complacently out of the office. A less inflexible woman would have brooded a little. She would have churned her anger toward Curtis into suspicion and fear or she would have snuffed back over old trails, recalling, reassuring, sentimentalizing. Mrs. Potter, had she been ordinary, would have made her glimpse of Charlie Harper an occasion for shuddering over their last meeting, on a roaring evening in Peachburg. From there she would have reviewed her flight to Corinth, the city so big that it could swallow old identities yet furnish pasture for new identities to graze. She might have mused on those trying years when Complexion Refineries, Inc., struggled in rustic vineyards and she and Curtis, with one chemist and a couple of salesmen, gloated over each cash order for a dozen bottles of Whiteine. Or Mrs. Potter, tapping out of the Nickajack Building to her motor, might have passed over the time of trial; comforted herself with the knowledge that last year six new states were "opened," making a total of thirty watered by her blessing to the Race; preened herself on her Paris dresses, her careful accent and her wealth and power as sole owner of a million-dollar corporation; arrogantly shrugged such cattle as Charlie Harper out of mind.

But Mrs. Genevieve Potter was not an ordinary woman. In her seven years in Corinth she had made herself rich because she had never cried over spilled milk. So in less than seven seconds from the moment she issued her orders concerning Peachburg trash, she had put those orders from her, knowing they would be obeyed, and was brooding in quite other directions.

The streets through which Mrs. Potter's motor slowly rolled were smooth and narrow, stuffed with traffic, over-shadowed by tall buildings. When her car stopped at a policeman's whistle, other cars surged crosswise, pedestrians scrambled for safety zones, horns blared and gongs clanged. Corinth seemed to swell lustier before her eyes. It was already 100,000; by 1925, said its boosters, it would be the Half Million City.

In all the 100,000, Mrs. Potter knew by sight perhaps a hundred persons and by name less than fifty. There were her executives at the office and the factory. At the hotel, there were the manager, the clerks and servants. There were, of course, her banker and her brokers. There was Josef the chauffeur, there were her maid and butler, and there were the men at the garage. There were, too, Laura and her husband and their friends. But that was all.

It was of this Mrs. Potter was thinking as her motor moved north along Cherokee Avenue. She could buy and sell every second man or woman treading those crowded sidewalks, yet of all the legion, not one lifted a respectful hat or waved a hand or spared her a glance in which was anything but impersonal envy.

Mrs. Potter's reflections were not tinged with self-pity. Her aloneness was simply a fact, one to which she had grown used, on which in times past she had congratulated herself, and which only recently had occurred to her as a fact not altogether satisfactory. Business was thriving. Less and less did the office, the shops, the beauty parlour, the movies, content her. Months ago she had confessed to herself that she wished she knew more people in a social way. The fact was that she didn't, and as the fact had grown more and more glaring, her restiveness had increased.

Laura and her husband had obscured the fact for a while. She had met them at the hotel when Eddie first came South to take the Tecumseh agency. The Tecumseh was a new car and hard pushing in a community sold on Fords and Buicks and Cadillacs, and Corinth was a new, hostile city to a girl born in Brooklyn and never before south of Asbury Park, N. J. Laura, knowing nobody and desperately lonely, scraped the acquaintance. Then Mrs. Potter, letting down a little for these Northern aliens, bought a Tecumseh sedan. After that she "ran with" Laura a lot, keeping up the friendship when the Kilpatricks moved from the expensive hotel to a small apartment. She and Laura shopped and sodaed and matineed together, drove into the country on fine days in Mrs. Potter's car, discussed clothes and movies and personal opinions and movies and clothes. Though Mrs. Potter never really told Laura anything about herself—vaguely she referred sometimes to Mr. Potter, "dead these five years"—she was, she supposed, Laura's "best friend" and Laura was hers.

Once in a while she went out with Laura and Laura's husband. She took them to a theatre, or they took her, or Eddie brought home one of the boys from the agency and they played bridge. Laura had an awful time teaching Genevieve bridge. "You've got to learn, Genevieve, everybody plays!" And Mrs. Potter, very humble, was truly grateful to Laura. Laura had taught Genevieve many things Genevieve didn't know—smart things from the North.

Sometimes she and Laura and Eddie went on "parties." In Summer they drove out to a road-house—"chicken houses," they called them in Corinth—and had fried chicken and hot biscuit and spaghetti and corn on the cob. If Eddie brought along one of the boys, there was usually a bottle of corn whisky. Everybody except Genevieve got very hilarious. Once Eddie was so drunk he couldn't drive the car and Genevieve had to drive it, and another time they were almost arrested. The agency boys thought Genevieve slow. She drank little and she didn't smoke at all and, though nothing seemed to shock her exactly, you never heard her tell a dirty story. She did call Eddie a son-of-a-bitch the night he couldn't drive, but it just shows you how mad she was. Really, she was too refined to be much fun.

Laura and Eddie didn't ask Genevieve on all their parties. She would have been a damper, and, besides, for all her dumbness about some things, they were a little afraid of her. That occasional hard look—and she was rich. "Who does she think she is?" Laura would complain privately to Eddie—"Mrs. Astor?"

Mrs. Potter, because she had nothing better to do, was on her way to Laura's now, and because Laura had nothing better to do, they would go to lunch somewhere or try a movie or drive out in the country. Watching the sidewalk crowds, Mrs. Potter wished she did have something better to do and that she didn't have to do it with Laura.

The sidewalk crowds were a fascinating aspect of Corinth, a composograph of the human city. Mrs. Potter could have foretold what their characteristics would be and how these would alter block by block every step of the way from the Nickajack to the Kilpatricks' apartment. She knew, as did everyone in Corinth, exactly where the colour of the downtown crowd would be dressy women and where women of the housewife and mother tradition; where men assumed preponderance, where these men would be clean and where dirty, where confident, where humble and where bold. Metropolitan though Corinth was, its every downtown block was a "woman block" or a "man block," a "white block" or a "nigger block," a block for powdered noses and conscious gait, or a block for pulling up the garter and belching. Going north along Cherokee Avenue, one would find the crowd less motley, even more definitely labelled. Near the Acropolis Hotel the last frowsy coat would suddenly disappear. In front of Brundage's, the crowd would consist of nobby young men lounging or seated in parked cars, and they would be reviewing young and pretty girls stepping past in faultless attire. If you hadn't shaved or if you had a run in your stocking, you crossed the street to avoid Brundage's. When Mrs. Potter entered Brundage's for a soda or a sundae, she often felt, though she might be smarter than the smart, that she had invaded a club to which she had no card.

After Brundage's the crowd would be less sacrosanct, but it would never lose the clubby quality entirely if you kept to Cherokee Avenue in the progress north. The shops, dwindling in number, the hotels, the fancy groceries, the drug stores, the churches, finally the fine old homes and the newer apartment monoliths—upon them all rested the air of being the property of a club, and the people who came out of these places, save for nursemaids and delivery boys, seemed to Mrs. Potter to be all members of this club. Mrs. Potter herself lived in the heart of the club's preserves, in the newest of Corinth hotels on a terraced corner far out from hurly-burly, and she walked into it and out of it as haughtily as any club member. Yet she never felt that she really belonged to the club. If someone had said to her, "Outside, you!—This is the Cherokee Terrace," she would have been amazed and enraged, but she would not have felt guiltless.

Of course, there was not one huge club in Corinth and, had it existed, Mrs. Potter would not actually have believed that all the people who came out of the houses, all the young men in front of Brundage's, all the pretty girls, belonged to it. There were several clubs in Corinth and around them crusted something called Society. It was a society founded on old families and old prestige rather than mere wealth, but even so it was a fairly elastic society and many people came and went in it with no more credentials than a pleasing appearance and sometimes not even that. Mrs. Potter knew Corinth had Society. She read in the papers about the dances at the clubs, the engagements and weddings, the names of those who went to New York and White Sulphur and Wrightsville Beach. She was not interested; she did not want to meet people. Society people, least of all. They antagonized her, she didn't analyse why. Absorbed in making money, she didn't miss knowing them. After all, she never had. It wasn't Corinth Society that made her feel like an invader sometimes; it wasn't Corinth Society she had been craving lately. It was human society—"I wish—I wish I knew more people in a social way."

Some of those women she saw in the shops and tearooms. They, too, wore good-looking clothes, had their own cars as she did, went to her hairdresser's and her chiropodist's. She overheard them talking, some she identified as Society women whose names she had read in the papers, and to her they seemed to be having a better time than she and Laura. Maybe they weren't. (Like them she had been to New York, seen shows, shopped on Fifth Avenue.) Maybe all they did was to go to matinees, drive around, play bridge. She bet she could play bridge as good as a lot of them. If she only knew a few, she could give a bridge party at the hotel. She bet she could give a party as swell as they could. But she wasn't going to give a party for Laura and her friends. Laura was so common sometimes. The way she flirted with that man in the Acropolis lobby. ...

Some of those men she saw in the office buildings—prosperous, jolly men. She'd known men like that before and they were fools, all right, like all men. You couldn't tell her anything about men. But they were entertaining, too. The men at her own office were afraid of her. Eddie's friends were no good. She had their number—a bottle of beer and try to bilk you on the room-rent. She wanted a man to treat the rich Mrs. Potter neither as the boss nor as Laura's friend, nor as the ex-landlady of a bawdy house. … That Curtis! A good thing to throw the fear of God into him once in a while.

Some of those fellows who hung around Brundage's. They were pretty young but she always did like the college boys. Something genteel about them even when they got soused and started rough houses. Who was that fellow who gave her his frat pin once and it turned out to be real emeralds? She wouldn't mind having a young fellow like that around, now that she was rich and cultured.

That was a handsome fellow in front of Brundage's a while ago, older than most, the one with the uniform on. Probably a training camp student. Corinth was suddenly full of them the last few days, young fellows in khaki and campaign hats, all going to be officers. …

It was terrible about the war, wasn't it? But sort of exciting, too, with people talking about the Germans invading us and Roosevelt going to take a division to France right away, and "The Star Spangled Banner" every time you sat down in a theatre and you had to get right up again. …

Mrs. Potter waited for Josef to open the door. Maybe—she thought as she tapped across the sidewalk—maybe she and Laura would try to get in that war movie, "The Beast of Berlin." But Norma Talmadge and Eugene O'Brien were in a new picture at the Elite.

"Hello," said Laura. "Oh, it's you! Come on in, Genevieve. Meet my friend, Mr. Metzger. Mr. Metzger's an old friend of mine from New York."

Laura looked a little flustered, thought Mrs. Potter, and Mr. Metzger looked a good deal like the man they had seen in the Acropolis lobby; but Mrs. Potter bowed politely and drawled "How do you do?" and sat down. Mr. Metzger broke an awkward silence.

"We were just about to have a smile. How about you, lady?"

Mrs. Potter's assent seemed to relieve Mr. Metzger. While Laura brought ice and glasses, he settled back with a jaunty air, produced a bottle and announced this was the best stuff south of the Smith and Wesson Line—"and I ought to know—bought it myself at Churchill's."

"Well, love and kisses," added Mr. Metzger.

"Oh, Churchill's!" thrilled Laura. "I've been to Churchill's!"

"Listen," interrupted Mr. Metzger, "you can't tell me anything about Churchill's, girlie. Why, I've been stewed in Churchill's more times than not."

Mr. Metzger told them about the last three times he was stewed in Churchill's, and another time when he was stewed in Churchill's with Eddie Foy, only he guessed that was Jack's; it was Frank Tinney he was stewed that time in Churchill's with, when Frank sent the funny telegram to George Cohan. He told them all about the funny telegram and said there wasn't anything you could tell him about Georgie Cohan.

"You know a lot of stage people, don't you, Mr. Metzger?" said Mrs. Potter. "Laura, did you know Norma Talmadge and Eugene O'Brien were at the Elite?"

"Eugene O'Brien?" countered Mr. Metzger. "Say, I knew Eugene O'Brien when he was nobody. I knew him when he was just a ham. Did I ever tell you about the time me and Eugene O'Brien were in Chicago? Say, girlie?"

Laura shook her head, so Mr. Metzger told them about that time and about another time in Denver when they threw the party for "The Pink Lady" company. "That was one grand little party," said Mr. Metzger.

"Are you an actor?" inquired Mrs. Potter.

"Me?" Mr. Metzger laughed loudly. "Me an actor? You tell her about me, girlie. Listen, I guess I know as many actors as anybody in America—and actresses!—I know my little old Broadway! But me an actor? How d'ye get that way?

"I'm a salesman," added Mr. Metzger. "I sell ink."

"I see," said Mrs. Potter. She wished, impatiently, Laura would not laugh at everything the man said. Was he really an old friend of Laura's? She'd seen too many Metzgers to believe that—travelling men—steady customers in the old days; now they beat the lonely evenings with the hotel manicurist or even better prospects in a city like Corinth. Well, if Laura was going in for that sort of thing—

"I'd like to see that picture at the Elite, wouldn't you?" she said to Laura.

"What?" Laura was bending over to look at Mr. Metzger's ring. "Wha' d'ju say, dear?"

"Let's all have another lil drink," said Mr. Metzger. "Come on, girlie. Shake 'em up!"

Mrs. Potter did not repeat her question. She rose, putting on her gloves.

"But you're not going!" exclaimed Laura.

"Aw, come on, girlie! have another little drink," urged Mr. Metzger.

Mrs. Potter finished putting on her gloves. She favoured Mr. Metzger with a long stare from her pale blue eyes.

"Thank you so much," she said. "Good-bye, dear!"

When the door had closed, Mr. Metzger pulled his lips into a grimace, after which he winked at Laura.

"Wow!" he exclaimed. "I wonder who took her marbles … Well, girlie?"

But Mrs. Potter, once more in her motor, was neither angry nor disgusted. She was bored. And along with bored a bit chagrined. Chagrined because of the consciousness that Laura had not wanted her to stay—Laura had desired her companionship even less than she had desired Laura's—Laura, too, must have been fed up with those interminable rides and luncheons—Laura had wanted to know someone else in a social way—and Laura had turned the trick. Just a drummer, a cheap pickup, but for a moment Mrs. Potter almost wished she could be as common as Laura.

Norma Talmadge and Eugene O'Brien were suddenly without meaning. Other people's lives—and not even real. Laura and the objectionable Mr. Metzger, by now embracing over the whisky bottle, at least were feeling emotions—what if they were sordid and fugitive? But she was out of that just as she was out of the movie. "All dressed up and no place to go," the man at the Orpheum had sung, and she had laughed … Well?

At the Cherokee Terrace she dismissed Josef and the car, but she did not go at once to her room. The main avenue of Corinth, with its trees and lawns and cavalcade of autos, was a pleasant vista at this hour on a Spring afternoon, and the veranda of the hotel, shaded by awnings and partially screened by shrubs and boxes of brilliant flowers, was a pleasant spot from which to watch the vehicles, the nursemaids and the spruce people whom Mrs. Potter thought of as all members of this club. She took a rocking-chair near a little fir tree and, gazing out at the life flashing past in the checkered sunshine, removed from the depths of her Paris bag a licorice "nigger baby" which, as if hiding a yawn, she popped into her mouth. After that, for a time, the slight frown between her eyes disappeared.

Mrs. Potter was still sitting there, rocking, an hour later, when the manager of the hotel quietly opened the door and with a gesture indicated the rocker to his companion, a large woman in white relieved by a floppy black hat and jet bangles that clicked whenever she breathed. The large woman agitated her face into what was meant to express silent but heartfelt gratitude, and at once descended on her prey.

"Mrs. Potter, isn't it? My dear Mrs. Potter, I'm sure you won't mind my speaking to you, we do so need help and it's a terribly worthy cause, indeed it is! I'm Mrs. Genelli, the chairman of the Committee for Armenian Relief—you know the Armenians?—and Mr. Sturgis—such a nice man!—suggested your name. We're having our tag day next Friday, the final drive to raise our quota, and of course Corinth simply must go over the top! It would be too terribly sad if we didn't. Of course everybody wants to do their bit, but with the war happening so suddenly and so many tag days and the Liberty Loan and the Red Cross and all, it's terribly difficult getting people. Not that I wouldn't have asked you among the *first* if I'd only thought! You do understand, don't you, dear? And it will be positively lovely if you only will!"

Gaping up into this torrent of words and the plump face from which they continued to pour, Mrs. Potter at length made out that this woman was asking her to join a committee to raise money, for whom she was completely at sea, since the woman had spoken of them as if they were some distressed family next door whom every nice person should know. Mrs. Potter rose, the more confused because she had been forced to swallow a licorice drop whole, but her initial impulse to cut the woman short when money was mentioned evaporated before a staggering light. Tag days? Charity? Why, only members of "the club" went in for that sort of thing!

"I'm sure, Mrs.—"

"Genelli, my dear, Mrs. Porter Genelli—I do believe we're neighbours. I'm right around the corner, you know."

She did know—that big grey house where the iron deer used to stand.

"Of course, Mrs. Genelli, if there's anything I can do—"

"Then you will serve! How lovely! I'm sure I'll be terribly grateful—and the Armenians, too, of course."

Mrs. Potter bowed. The Porter Genellis was a name familiar through newspaper paragraphs. The Armenians she couldn't place.

"I'll be delighted, Mrs. Genelli."

The flow of the torrent had ceased momentarily while Mrs. Genelli, having gained her point, caught breath. In the pause Mrs. Potter struck the iron with characteristic sagacity.

"About what I'm to do, now—Mrs. Genelli, would you like some tea?"

"My dear Mrs. Potter—how lovely!"

A stranger in Corinth, observing the two ladies cross the lobby, would have seen in one of them only a stout woman in a floppy hat who panted and wore too many ornaments. About the younger, however, was something besides her smart costume— there was an air, undoubtedly an air.

CHAPTER NINE
CAMPAIGN

THE CITY of Corinth went over the top for starving Armenia. Tag Day was a remarkable success. Remarkable because, as Mrs. Porter Genelli for weeks had moaned to her husband, you really couldn't expect people to bother about the Armenians now! Two months before, when she had accepted the chairmanship, it wasn't so bad. The atrocities were all over the newspapers and that girl, Katya-something-or-other, had appalled an audience at the Civic Club. Her mother chopped up before her eyes!—it was too terrible. And, in spite of the talk that Corinth was sick of campaigns—buy a bale of cotton, adopt a French orphan, help a Belgian refugee, knit socks for soldiers, to say nothing of the regular tag days for the day nursery and the old ladies' home and the free library and the tuberculosis clinic—in spite of the fact that she had done her bit in all of these, Mrs. Genelli had shouldered the Armenians. And then—what a tragedy!—her plans just perfected when America got into the war. Overnight—camps, conscription, Liberty Loan, Red Cross, food conservation, war gardens, preserve or perish, canteen girls, release-a-man-for-service, carry-your-own- package, teach-English-to-foreigners, save-peachstones- and-win-the-war—it was *our* war, everyone in it up to the neck, and the Armenians were just another bunch of wops—who cared how many the Turks massacred? No wonder Mrs. Genelli wept because she must carry on.

And a triumph, after all! There had been a dismal moment in the shank of the afternoon with the checkup of the morning workers, when Mrs. Genelli had cried, "We can't! We simply can't! I'll wire New York our quota *must* be reduced!" The committee had conferred solemnly over Mrs. Genelli's expiring obligation, with none seeming ready save to call it a death. And then Mrs. Potter—that duck of a Mrs. Potter! …

Genevieve thoroughly enjoyed Armenian Tag Day. She rose early and put on her most becoming frock, for she was resolved that no friend of Armenia should look nicer than she. The members of the committee she did not fear—she had met them twice at luncheons—but today there would be young girls, too, the sort who frequented Brundage's and shrieked enchantingly to young men across yards of floor.

One of these, Miss Mary Wimbish, she called for in her car at eight o'clock, Mrs. Genelli having made the arrangements and imposed on Miss Wimbish the duty of recruiting other girls for Genevieve's group—"dear Mrs. Potter has been *so* kind, but she knows very few people—yes, dear, a Northerner, but *terribly* nice!—really, just a girl herself—a widow—so sad, isn't it?"

Waiting outside the Wimbish home on Magnolia Drive in the pearly May morning, Genevieve knew a thrill uncaptured since that day, fourteen years before, when Cora Potts set out to dazzle Peachburg with her 18-karat tooth. Only last week, Wimbishes and Genellis were too remote even to envy; now she was practically the same as one of them and the taste of the sensation was butter and sugar in her soul. The sudden advent of Miss Mary Wimbish cut short these agreeable reflections.

Miss Wimbish appeared in a flutter of organdy and woe.

"Oh, gee, Mrs. Potter, I'm so mad I could pop! Some'n awful's happened! Nancy Ann Morgan just this minute 'phoned me she can't come, she's sick or some'n, and Mildred Buck who was spendin' the night with her, she can't come, too, 'cause she thinks she ought to stay with Nancy Ann, and I only got two other girls and—it's just awful!"

Gazing into Miss Wimbish's face where it despaired above the car window, Mrs. Potter for a moment did not speak. She was not so much thinking as she was undergoing a reflex shaped by old experience of feminine truancy, old knowledge of what to do when ladies suddenly fell ill. Her response was without precedent in Corinth social etiquette, but it was to win her, wholly unintended, the awed attention of at least one clique in Corinth society.

"Does Nancy Ann live far?" inquired Mrs. Potter. "She might be feeling better. I was thinking," she added softly, "we might drive by there."

"Yes'm," agreed Miss Wimbish. She was too astounded to demur.

Ten minutes later, facing two young ladies in negligee breakfasting heartily on waffles, Miss Wimbish wailed:

"I couldn't help it, could I? I *knew* there wasn't anything the matter with you all, but she *made* me do it. You gotta come, Nancy Ann! You dash into your clothes right this minute!"

"But we gotta date!"

"I don't care if you gotta million dates—you *gotta* come, both of you! There's some'n weird about that Mrs. Potter—she *knows* you're not sick and I'll bet she'll make you good'n sorry if you *don't* come. There's some'n about her—you come on, now, this minute!"

They came.

And so, throughout the day, from the distribution of the little buckets at headquarters until shadows fell long across the sidewalks where the Misses Wimbish, Buck, Morgan, Elton and Pettigrew still assailed their quarry in the name of starving

Armenia, the spell of Genevieve Potter ruled her minions. She herself was insatiable. She led the charge, she spurred the flagging, she telephoned hourly reports, she dispatched Josef for more tags, she made change like a bank teller, she checked returns to the penny, she paused only for a sandwich, she was everywhere every minute with her eyes, her electric voice, her undiminished smile.

"Now, girls!" And Miss Morgan forgot all about 'phoning her date, Miss Buck had no second for flirtation, Miss Wimbish braced gentlemen with a pertness her mother would have swooned to see. "Now, girls!" And half-eaten salads were left on plates. "Now, girls!" And those hateful tags were brandished again, those weary pipings for Armenia rehymned. "Now, girls!" Terrified Miss Pettigrew cast temptation from her. Bridge debts were one thing, but the argus eye of that woman was another.

Mrs. Potter, in happy ignorance that hers was one of the least choice corners and nobody expected her to bring in many sheaves, did not know that she was building a reputation as a go-getter. She was, simply enough, having a grand time. She hadn't had such a grand time since the Elks' convention in 1909, when The Mansion raked in fifteen hundred dollars on a single Saturday night. She who had gloried in Saturday nights and who for seven years had been limited to whiphanding a few men, took to Tag Day like a colt to clover. The crowd, the girls, money to get, tough customers to bulldoze, easy marks to take—it was old times. She revelled without a thought that she was a wonder or suspecting in the least why.

Two incidents of the busy day stood out for her. A familiar face bobbed, a familiar voice gasped, "Genevieve!" She said to Laura, "How do you do?" and cut Mr. Metzger dead. Laura's expression wavered between surprise and mirth, and Genevieve did not propose to be laughed at. She trilled, "You'll excuse me, won't you? Mrs. Porter Genelli's on the 'phone." Then—"Mary, dear, will you give these persons tags?" If Laura didn't get that double-barrelled load of high society, she didn't know Laura.

The other incident, though not so tasty, stuck longer in Genevieve's memory. Nancy Ann Morgan screamed suddenly, "Nee-yul! Nee-yul!" A young man in dark blue and a grey hat seesawed perilously through the angry traffic. When he reached Miss Morgan's side, Mrs. Potter was not a foot away.

"Neal, you big old crazy! Why'n't you pay any mind to me on the street? I'm gonna make you buy *all* my tags!"

The young man grinning down at the girl was, thought Mrs. Potter, oddly flustered. She wondered where she had seen him before.

"Every last one of 'em," continued Miss Morgan, "and you're lucky I haven't got but—lemme see—four, five—twelve! Here y'are, mister, dollar a tag and I'm givin' you a special rate!"

"Have a heart, Nancy Ann. I'm busted."

Miss Morgan gurgled deliciously.

"Don't fib to me, honey! Ev'body knows you're makin' gobs of money workin' for that crazy old nigger medicine swindle."

The young lady's voice was high, and when she had spoken, the feeblest of smiles succeeded her young man's grin, a dark red climbed above his collar and stayed there, while his glazing eyes stared desperately beyond hers.

"Why, Neal! You mad at me, honey?"

Suddenly Mrs. Potter's memory clicked.

"You will buy a tag, won't you, Mr. Carver?" she warbled past Nancy Ann's shoulder.

"Oh, yes!—yes, indeed!" He was fumbling in his pocket, his confusion no less for the saving interruption. "Here, Nancy Ann, here's ten—I owe you two dollars—gimme those things—"

And muttering something about pressing engagements, Mr. Carver backed away with his tags, the red still hot in his ears and all that was left of his week's salary in the astonished Miss Morgan's bucket.

"Well, I'll be gosh-damned! 'scuse me, Mrs. Potter, but I never saw Neal Carver act that-a-way in all my life!"

Mrs. Potter laughed.

"I thought he was a very nice boy."

"Oh, sure, he's nice enough—ev'body knows the Carvers. But did you ever? Just 'cause I talked about his crazy old nigger job!—You reckon he's crazy?"

To which Mrs. Potter murmured that she hoped not; he really seemed nice whatever his work was.

At five o'clock Genevieve called it a day. One thousand and fourteen dollars and ninety-six cents, she calculated, had been raised by her squad. Enough to feed forty Armenians for a month and a half. Or was it one and a half Armenians for forty months? She really couldn't remember. But Mrs. Genelli would know. Mrs. Genelli had all those figures in little books and could dazzle you with them, even if occasionally she got mixed up and said millions where she might mean thousands or hundreds. Genevieve hoped Mrs. Genelli would not be displeased. Yet she was apprehensive. Forty wasn't a lot of Armenians or even a lot of months. Reflectively she added four cents from her own purse to even the total, and reluctantly she dismissed her workers.

"You've been splendid, girls, splendid! We must all see each other soon. Now give me your addresses. ..."

Yearning to give the wrong ones, they gave the right To "see her soon"—frightful prospect!—"Listen, Mary Wimbish, if you ever put that woman onto me again, I'll kill you, child! She's kinder cute and I'll swear to goodness, I can't help likin' her, but she works too hard! My goodness, if I did this ev'ry day, I'd be a wreck—just a crazy old wreck!"

Genevieve tapped wearily up the steps of the Acropolis Hotel. Upstairs, in the pine room, a dozen ladies sat around a table. Here, from week to week, Kiwanians were wont to shout happily and college boys rattled the chandeliers with gleeful harmonies. But the dozen ladies, facing a litter of unsold tags and a heap of silver and dirty bills, presented no such congenial picture. They hated each other silently. They were hot and tired and sick to death of every Armenian girl ravished and every Armenian baby butchered, and at least one of them, watching a hand scratch numerals on white paper, was on the edge of tears.

"I am *not* wrong, Aline!" snapped the lady with the pencil. "Eleven thousand, four hundred and thirty-two dollars and nine cents—and not a red penny more! There!"

Mrs. Genelli lifted a handkerchief already damp.

"Oh, dear!" she moaned, and no other sound broke the funereal silence save Mrs. Genelli's sniff.

"Oh, dear, what *will* we do?"

Mrs. Genelli was waiting vainly for an answer to that question when a newcomer entered. Madam Chairman smiled mechanically; the rest glared. They neither liked nor disliked this Mrs. Potter; they would have glared at anybody. Still Mrs. Potter felt rather biffed.

She sat down.

"How much, dear?" mourned Mrs. Genelli.

"A thousand and fifteen dollars," said Mrs. Potter.

Coos of wonder and congratulation—"We never *dreamed!*"— "How marvellous!"—"Lovely!"—"How in the world did you— why, my dear, we put you down for only six hundred!"

Most gratifying. Most agreeable. Mrs. Potter steamed in a little fog of approbation.

A voice snapped: "And *that's* only eleven thousand, eight hundred and forty-seven and one cent. The quota's twenty thousand. Nearly nine thousand short"

Nine thousand short! Genevieve was amazed. The announcement fell on her ears with a shock out of all proportion to the sum. She had expected twenty thousand to be given for the Armenians as a matter of course. She had believed all these campaigns went over the top with a bang. Didn't the newspapers boast always—"the great heart of Corinth"—"immediate response"—"heavy oversubscription"? Her only fear had been that they would be ashamed of her, and now she was ashamed of them. They had put her down for but six hundred, and the thousand she had thought "paltry" led, they were saying, the entire list. What was the matter with this bunch? What had they been doing all day while she hustled? A lot of loafers and pikers—cold-footed quitters! that's what they were. She despised and resented them with their coos and their ineffectiveness and their supercilious refusal to know they were that way. Why, a good honest street-walker could spot them cards and spades when it came to real work and getting the coin. Give her the old gang at The Mansion for half a day and she bet she could save every heathen in Asia. This crowd just mewed around and secretly rejoiced that the thing was a flop. All but Mrs. Genelli, the poor fool, acting like a cry-baby! Nine thousand, after all, wasn't so much. She'd like to show them a few figures—make 'em sit up and then knock 'em cold. Suddenly Genevieve chuckled at an idea so dazzling yet so simple that she all but loved these deadly females it would annihilate.

"This isn't funny, Mrs. Potter," snorted the lady with the pencil.

"I'm sorry." They saw, to their amazement, that Mrs. Potter was smiling as she leaned forward to examine the calculations, and they were scandalized that she could be so heartless before poor Aline.

"We need eight thousand, one hundred and fifty-two dollars and ninety-nine cents, don't we?" inquired Mrs. Potter. "I'll be very happy to write a check for ten thousand as my contribution for the day."

When they stared unbelievingly, when they still could not speak as Mrs. Potter opened her bag, when one began to clap furiously, when the others joined and the clapping exploded into voices all talking at once, when Mrs. Potter signed the check with a casual hand, when Mrs. Genelli let loose floodgates upon Mrs. Potter's bosom, when each of them came up and enveloped her and called her "darling" and "my dear," Genevieve tasted to the full the startled envy and the jealous malice they bore her, and the taste was sweet. The knowledge of it soothed the last pang she might have felt over parting with her thousands, and had she but known that five of the ladies telephoned Mrs. Genelli within the hour, advising Madam Chairman to cash the check at once, her day would have been complete.

In Corinth homes that night, ignorant males exasperated their womenfolk past endurance. "You never even *heard* of her? I thought you knew *everybody* in Corinth! You're always boasting about it. I wonder how many *men* in this town could sign a check for ten thousand dollars!" Only one or two had meagre facts. Mr. Pendleton, the banker, recalled a Mrs. Potter as one of his biggest depositors—in the proprietary medicine business, he believed—and Mr. Drayton, of Drayton & Barnes, real estate, knew Mrs. Potter as a shrewd and heavy buyer of tenements and suburban property. "She'll clear a hundred thousand on that Laurel Heights development, and that ain't a patch on what she's made in the last three years. Believe me, this is the first time I ever heard of her *giving* anything away!"—"But who *is* she?" That, neither Pendleton nor Drayton nor any other could say, so neatly had Genevieve Potter eluded those forgotten shadows, Thelma LaMont and Cora Potts.

Genevieve herself spent an evening in repose none could say she had not earned. The feet that had borne so much for Armenia sloughed their agony on a cushion of silk, and their owner among many pillows let fall a head in which, for once, no ambition buzzed.

Only one caller disturbed her self-content. Curtis Rowlett, making his regular report, had reached within a few items of the end when Genevieve sat up from the chaise-longue.

"There's a man in the office named Carver. What does he get?"

"I don't know." Curtis fidgeted at the intrusion of the question. "Fifty a week, I think."

"Raise him to a hundred. Tell him I ordered it. No—don't. Tell him you regard his work as promising and you recommended him for a raise."

"But he's only been with us a few weeks. He's just a kid. He'll be getting more than Blake—almost as much as Meeker. What's the big idea?"

Genevieve yawned.

"I said—raise him to a hundred."

Used to some flat and short orders from his President, Curtis still burned with resentment. That snob Carver—despised him from the first—Thelma was cuckoo—not going to stand for it. He shifted in his chair, loosening the tight wrinkles of his trousers.

"You're making a big mistake. This Carver's no good. Just a pretty boy. He's liable to leave you flat any day. Shouldn't wonder if he enlisted, got into one of these officers' training camps. He's that kind. A society bird. He's got pull and he could get a commission easy. Why make everybody else sore?"

Genevieve looked at Curtis with a dull flare far back of her eyes. He could not know what she was thinking, he believed he had infuriated her, and he winced from what was coming.

But Genevieve relaxed against her pillows.

"Shut up," she said. "And get along. I'm tired of listening to you. There's one other thing. I drew a check today to the Committee for Armenian Relief. It's a little less than ten thousand dollars. Telephone the bank before nine in the morning and tell them to honour it without a lot of stink."

Curtis got up. He would have liked to hit her. He would have liked to go over to the couch where she lolled so indolently, her ankles crossed, her arms lax, the silk tight across her breast, and strike her in the mouth. Ten thousand dollars to Armenian Relief! She must be off her nut. This—and a hundred a week to that Carver kid. What did she think she was doing? The business wouldn't stand it. Oh, yes, it would—he knew that. He, of all people, knew it. All right—let her have her own way. The durn tart, she hadn't changed much, had she? Yes, she had—oh, yes, she had, lying there like a society dame. He couldn't go over and hit her. He couldn't, now, go over and put his arm around her, put his mouth on hers, put his hand across the tight drawn silk, as any man might have, once, who had the price. Not that he wanted to—now, huh? Plenty of that stuff around. But suppose he did? What would she do—now? Bust him one? No—she wouldn't do that. She'd changed, he knew she wouldn't let him touch her. Afraid? Rats! Who wanted to touch her? He'd like to hit her, though—hit her, kick her, curse her.

CHAPTER TEN
NEAL

THE STREET on which the Carvers lived was so old that the sidewalk held the nick dug by a Yankee bullet. When Neal turned into the street, walking home from work, he looked down and marked the nick and remembered how he had cut out the bullet when he was six, and though, when he looked up again, newness and change were all around, he saw the Carver house ahead, still old, and it seemed to him the street had been always as it was and would be so always. Fashion had moved away, northward, and progress had moved in with stores and garages and walls built stone to the sidewalk stone. There were no trees in the block now but the sycamores in the Carver yard, and even these were bedraggled, with the Carver house showing through their branches a dirty grey. Yet to Neal, going up the walk, the house seemed to stretch a hand, and the creak in the broken steps was friendly.

He hung his hat on the hall rack. His mother would be in the back somewhere, preparing supper, and he should go and kiss her. He should put his arm around her with the exact degree of pressure she would expect, and he should smile. That would tell her all was well, whether it was or not, and then he could be alone for a little in his own room.

But he wanted to be there now, to sit in the dusk with his inanimate belongings around him. He went to his room. ...

"They passed me slick," said Jack Burr. "That Colonel's a card! I had to guess wild on the eye-chart. 'M-Q- B-D-E,' I said. He didn't bat an eye. 'M-O-P-D-F, you say?' he said. 'Is that what you said?'—'Yes, sir,' I said, and he wrote me down perfect!" Jack Burr's bad eyes had laughed behind his lenses. And so Jack Burr was going off to the war. ...

New faces in his old office, the city room of the Blade. "Where's McDonald?"—"Oh, didn't you know? He got in the Marines." Old McDonald in the Marines! And Melton and Pace and little Eddie Driscoll in the first officers' training camp; they would have commissions in another two months. New faces— and on the old, as he looked at them, an unspoken question. ...

Uniforms in front of Brundage's. Whipcord and puttees and swagger sticks. A lot of chaps he never saw before; others he knew well, had known always. "Hello, Neal, how's the kid?" Their voices rang hearty. He joined in the talk, the laughter. Was it his fancy there was a chill here, the unspoken question on these faces, too? ...

Well, there would be the draft soon, and he would go up with the other conscripts—"selectmen," they called them! He would go up with the married men and the fathers and the workers and the misfits like Barney Gillam, with his cork leg. Some of them would be eager and some would be afraid, and he would sit with them until his turn came. Probably old Doctor Wayne would examine him, and he would be found sound in wind and limb. Or would they ask him questions first? He hoped Dr. Wayne would not ask the questions, for his grandfather had been Dr. Wayne's colonel at Chancellorsville. "Do you claim any dependents, Carver?"—*Claim!* As though dependents could be only a loop-hole for slackers! ...

He got up and switched on the light. On the bed he laid out shirt and studs, socks and a black tie. The conventional garments seemed to huddle away from him. Half the men tonight would be in khaki. If only he had the courage, or cowardice, to duck it! But to duck the dance was to duck them all—Brundage's, McDonald, Jack Burr, the war.

He heard his mother's voice, calling him, and he went downstairs.

Supper was served in the dining-room where, in Neal's childhood, crystal candelabra shimmered on the sideboard and the table was all white and silver and roses. Now the room was dingy. Long ago the broken candelabra had found the ash heap and never been replaced. Some of the furniture and all the silver were sold after Mr. Carver's bankruptcy. Scratches on the chairs. One had a broken arm which Uncle Gates Carver periodically tried to stick with glue. It never stuck. Uncle Gates would complain bitterly that the house was going to the devil, but he never stooped to remedy things by taking the small jobs old friends offered. The Carvers of his generation were brought up to give jobs, not take them.

Uncle Gates and Neal sat down while Mrs. Carver brought in the dishes—chops and hominy and new peas and a salad—and Uncle Gates discussed gustily the news he had gleaned that day from hotel reading racks.

The British had captured Bullecourt and British warships were bombarding Zeebrugge. The Germans were reported falling back all along the Arras front. A Zeppelin, crossing the North Sea, was destroyed by British seaplanes. "I tell you," said Uncle Gates, "if we don't hurry, the war will be over. Why don't they listen to Roosevelt? Give him his head and he'd have a division in France before you could say 'Jack Robinson!' Did you see what Billy Sunday said? He said, 'I'd like to go with Roosevelt if I couldn't do anything but black his boots!' "

"Why doesn't he go, then?" asked Neal. "He's rich enough."

"Too old, my boy." Uncle Gates bayoneted his chop as though it had been a Hun. "The young fellows must carry the flag this time. Fellows like this Sergeant Empey. Have you read his pieces in the Blade? Thrilling! Over the top with a cheer and devil take the Boche! Makes you itch to be in the trenches. I see where some actor in New York—old fellow—has agreed to pay ten dollars a week to a soldier's wife till the war's over. If I had the money, by gad! I'd pay a dozen."

"You can make ten dollars a week."

Neal wanted to say it, but across the table were his mother's eyes pleading—the watching, fearful eyes he was always fleeing. He picked silently at his food.

"Aren't you hungry, Neal?"

"Sure I am, Mother."

He wished she wouldn't keep after him so. His appetite, his looks, what he wore, how he slept, where he was going, whether he wanted anything. Of course, she had always been that way. It was awful—sheer, crazy morbidness—to feel that he was being watched and guarded because she was his dependent. She used to ask him what he was thinking about; she did not ask that any more.

He looked up and each surprised the secret in the other's gaze. Neal's fell miserably. He felt ashamed, as though he had threatened a dog waiting submissively for the blow.

"Anything about Dr. Waite in the papers, Gates?" asked Mrs. Carver.

Murder freshened the conversation. While the two older people talked of the man in Sing Sing's death house, Neal's thoughts twisted back to his own shackles. Again he debated: shall I tell them? Once spoken, no blinking the significance of his news. He could see his mother's face light up, Uncle Gates expanding with hopes of carfare and cigars; hear their exclamations—"Neal!

How marvellous! Why didn't you tell us before?" Yet it would be so easy to say nothing. A little while and he could enter the second training camp. They gave you a hundred a month and subsistence. Couldn't they all live on that? In the meantime he could save nearly five hundred before he quit his job. And if he got a captain's commission, if he was careful, if they were careful, if Mrs. Carver scrimped a little more—he realized, suddenly, that his mother's plate held only hominy and peas and he choked.

"Mother! You must take my other chop."

"No, I don't want it. Really, dear, I shouldn't eat meat."

What was a hundred a month compared to a hundred a week? Why, he could give her servants, a car, clothes—and now she couldn't buy lamb chops! He spoke quickly.

"I got a raise today. ..."

When Mr. Rowlett had told him that morning, he couldn't believe it. The sum was incredible. But the Vice-President had repeated the magic numerals. "Just one thing, Carver—don't mention this around the office, not even to Meeker." Of course he wouldn't; he was exceedingly grateful; he hadn't dreamed— "That's all right," the Vice-President had cut him short. "Fact is, I've been watching your work, and I decided to recommend you for a raise. That's all." He had walked out in a glorious daze, too excited for the full implications of his luck to sink home. A hundred dollars a week! Why, he hadn't expected to make that much for years! Mr. Rowlett was a great fellow; Neal was ashamed of every suspicion harboured against him, every quaver of revolt against the job. If this was what writing testimonials got you. ... Up to the windows of the eleventh floor of the Nickajack Building, out of a street suddenly hushed of traffic, had come a new sound, the steady thrupp, thrupp, thrupp of many heels striking in unison. It was only for a moment. Then the files had passed without even music or a cheer, and clatter resumed where crowds had stood silently, watching them go by. But in that still interval, with the wind bringing him what he could not see, Neal had stopped dead on the way to his typewriter, a fist clenching his heart. ...

"... Raise of fifty dollars."

"Why, Neal! ..."

They were exclaiming, they were laughing and crying, they were doing all the things he had known they would do. Once, how proud he would have been! He pushed back his chair.

"Please, Mother, I've got to dress. There! You mustn't cry. Anyone would think I'd been fired instead of promoted. I can't eat anything more. Please. I've got to go. I've got to go. ..."

At least, Berenice hadn't been there. Time enough tomorrow to tell her that now she could buy her canteen worker's uniform.

CHAPTER ELEVEN
SATURDAY AFTERNOON

Mrs. POTTER was playing bridge at the country club.

"Three spades," said the woman on her right.

"Three no trumps," said Mrs. Potter.

"Double."

The queen of spades led, and Mrs. Potter spread her hand—jack of diamonds, five and trey, the lone club, seven hearts, spade king and deuce. She relaxed, gazing at the other tables in unashamed thankfulness for time out. So far, the party had been the worst ordeal of her life.

A moan surprised her—composed of hysteria and the death rattle. She noted that it came from her partner, whose eyes were fixed on the board as though Mrs. Potter had just dealt a rattlesnake. Good Lord! What had she done now?

"I believe Work is still advising the takeout with a seven-card major, dear," said Mrs. Potter's partner, and smiled at her toothily.

Work? Takeout? Mrs. Potter's fingers itched to pull hair while she watched ace fall on queen and king, and the spade lead returned. She knew she had blundered, though she didn't know how—Laura *always* said bid no trumps if you had the suit stopped—and she knew she had been insulted, though the method of insult foiled her. Furthermore, she was sure it was the fourth or fifth time she had been insulted this afternoon and each time too adroitly for her to spit back. These women! That was the hell of it—nasty in the nasty-nice way you could meet only with a freezing smile. And she was sick of smiling freezingly. Oh, for ten minutes with a few beer bottles! The guest of honour could have made hash out of Mrs. Porter Genelli's bridge party, yet she must smile and take it—smile and take it as she had been taking it ever since the day after she saved Armenia.

It had begun that day with the newspapers. There was the announcement right enough—"Corinth Over the Top, Tag Day A Triumph"—and Mrs. Genelli's picture on the front page. Mrs. Potter's eyes had galloped down the column to the list of names. And then the first sour shock—her own was not among them!

Of course Mrs. Genelli had telephoned frantic apologies, and of course the "oversight" had been corrected in the afternoon papers. But by then the flavour had gone with the ten thousand dollars, leaving Mrs. Potter sulkily resentful that she, who had pulled the fat from the fire, had no picture of herself to clip and lay beside the yellow smudge, "Prominent Society Woman at Dog Show," among the recipes for reducing and clippings from "Vogue."

The bridge party was Mrs. Genelli's gesture of atonement. She had pondered long before giving it. She knew dear Mrs. Potter was hurt—how unfortunate that Nanny Overstreet had "forgotten" to include her name with the rest! She knew, too, there was talk, that Mrs. Werner Sims had said Mrs. Potter was a nobody from Brooklyn or one of those places, that others were saying Mrs. Potter got her money from a very queer sort of business. But timid Mrs. Genelli did hate to hurt people, and a lot of businesses were queer these days, weren't they? Look at the Candlers in Atlanta—Coca-Cola. Look at those rich what's-their-names in Birmingham—toilet paper, wasn't it? And the Wrigleys with their chewing gum and the Fords with Fords. Yet people had broken their necks to meet Henry Ford when he stopped in Corinth last year, and probably there were nice people in Brooklyn. So Mrs. Genelli had decided on her bridge—"to meet Mrs. Genevieve Potter."

The guest prize cost fifteen dollars. It cannot be said, however, that Mrs. Potter got full return for her ten thousand.

How was she to know that the slights and snubs were founded on nothing more sinister than mere envy of a woman who could toss away money at will? How was she to tell that those insults across the table were prompted as much by her diamonds as they were by her poor bridge? Or, terrified that rumours of her past were destroying her, to guess that even then the gods were preparing new steps for her ascent?

"Three down," said Mrs. Potter's partner. "So sorry!"

"Don't break your heart," said Mrs. Potter, whose culture had begun to skip a few beats.

Seven miles away, in the office of Corson & Corson, the realtors, big business was about to honour Mrs. Potter. Big business had taken up the cross of patriotism, big business was marching as to war, big business was come together on a Saturday afternoon to consider the item of half a million dollars from Corinth for the American Red Cross, and big business was stumped for patriots willing and able to tote the load. They had made Jim Corson local chairman, hung it on him despite his protests that a Three-Minute Man, and captain of a Liberty Loan team to boot, is more than doing his bit for his country. After all, begged Jim Corson, a patriot can't let his business go blooey, war or no war; after all, silently recalled each member of the delegation, Jim Corson is cleaning up on cantonment sites, he can afford to be a patriot. You're elected, Jim—and that was that. But a woman chairman— what to do, what to do? Thousands of willing women in Corinth. Willing to be Red Cross nurses. Willing to be canteen workers.

Willing to bare their breasts to the Huns, cut their hands off, slave themselves sick in any cause that had to do with the war. But war was a business, patriotism was a business, raising half a million dollars for the Red Cross was a business demanding a doer and a leader among women. Painful experience in drives innumerable had taught the big business men of Corinth that their women were beautiful and charming and cajoling, but that in business they were little children lost in thick forests or wandering in what they conceived to be delightful daisy fields. There were exceptions, a few, but already these were enlisted to the hilt in war work. There were volunteers a-plenty for the ranks, but there was none fitted to be general. And then someone mentioned the name of a Mrs. Potter, and told how singlehanded she had put Corinth over the top for Armenia, and big business did a rapid calculation; if a subaltern is good for ten thousand in a feeble cause, how much will she kick in as Madam Chairman of a Red Cross campaign?

"I never heard of her before," said Jim Corson, "but she sounds like a sucker and a worker, both!"

At the country club, Mrs. Potter's partner was saying, "It's a seven rubber. We stay here, *but*—we change partners!"

Many miles nearer Mrs. Potter than the office of Corson & Corson, two young men played golf. When they reached the eighteenth tee, one of them stepped back from his ball and for a moment rested on his driver as a sentinel might rest upon a gun and gaze out from his post Ahead of him was the lake, sad with green and bronze shadows, the green slope on the far side, the white clubhouse among green trees, and the red west. Behind him, the sun still painted golden ripples across the fairways, and white figures moved tinily against light green and dark. Sound chimed here; the lap of water, the faint crack of a drive, they were ordered to the quiet sweep of green that breathed with nothing between it and the sky.

"A pretty sweet old dump," said the young man with the driver. "I hate to leave it. Well—my last swing for a long time, Neal."

He drove. The ball was a black dot against the sunset, then a sudden white dribble into nothing.

"On the green," said Neal.

He followed Owen across the little bridge, acutely conscious of the clump of their heels and of Owen's back just in front of him. Owen's neck was red brown and the muscles of his shoulders showed flat and hard where they stuck to his wet shirt. The calves of his legs, below the knickers, swung along hard and rhythmically. Neal thought how he would remember Owen's back always and how Owen's legs would look, swinging along hard and rhythmically, in puttees. He wished he could say to Owen something of what he felt, but of course he couldn't. They must walk together, perhaps for the last time, and be silent except for the hollow clump of their heels. For Owen was going to Quantico tomorrow, and Owen had been Neal's best and closest friend for eighteen years.

They did not stop when they had holed out. If either would have delayed for an instant, for a last word, for a last look, he did not show it. They moved almost hurriedly toward the clubhouse and while they bathed and dressed in the locker room, even while Owen poured drinks from a gin bottle, while they talked to other men about scores, each was quick at what he did as though furtively he watched the other and feared the other would think he prolonged the moments.

Owen, dressed first, fumbled over things in his locker.

"Hi—Jim!"

The Negro rubber waited.

"Guess I won't have much use for these—"

"Yas, suh. Thanky, suh!"

The Negro asked no questions—he, too, knew Owen was going away to war.

"Guess I won't have much use for these, either, Neal.—Make you a present. They're good clubs."

"In your hat," said Neal. "I'll take care of them till you get back."

He picked up the bag and swung it across his shoulder with his own.

"I think I'll breeze along, Owen."

"Not staying for the dance? Better have another drink, anyway."

"No," said Neal. "I've got a date. Guess I'll breeze along. It was nice of you to have me out, Owen."

"Rot," said Owen. He rose briskly. "Well, old socks—"

Their eyes met. Their hands.

"Good luck, kid," said Neal.

"Thanks, old-timer. You, too."

Neal went downstairs without looking back. Some sort of women's shindig was breaking up below and the club was full of gabble. He slipped through a side door into the dusk, walking to the end of the driveway. A hundred feet farther on the trolley would stop, and people already were there, waiting. But he preferred to wait here, by the big pillars. He didn't want to talk to anybody. If he were a girl, he would be crying now, he supposed. A girl would cry tonight because Owen was going away and she would be left behind, and that, of course, was why he wanted to cry, partly because Owen was going away, but mostly because he was left behind. Like a girl. The tears he could not cry ached through his whole body.

He was like that when Mrs. Potter's car slowed for the exit.

"Stop, Josef. ... Mr. Carver—"

He got in automatically. A lift was a lift and anything better than the trolley crowded with people he knew.

Mrs. Potter's own mood was not happy. All her life, which was the life of an unimaginative and simple person, she had wanted precise things, and because she was unimaginative, she had gotten them by simple methods unencumbered with doubts of right and wrong. Now, however, she wanted something not precisely clear to her. It was not wealth, for she was wealthy. It was not mere respectability, one of the few unprecise things she had desired. She was respectable. If it was social prestige and power, Mrs. Potter did not think of it in those terms; she thought, instead, of hurting and humiliating the women who had humiliated her and she did not know a simple way to do it. Leaving the club alone in her Packard expressed her desire in a way, and picking up Neal Carver was an impulse related to it. Neal belonged to the enemy—well, she would "show" them by riding off with him. It was something, anyway.

Mrs. Potter practised conversation. As the car sped along, she spoke of the country club, the bridge party and the ladies, and though her words indicated her long familiarity with Corinth society and her good-humoured tolerance of its shortcomings, her manner was so airy that an attentive listener might have decided that Mrs. Potter was either a fool or talking to hide some secret worry. She herself must have sensed a hollowness in her gay monologue, for she stopped, she waited for a rejoinder, and when her companion was silent, she turned to him in a fright that he had fallen asleep.

Neal sat with his eyes straight ahead and a rigidity in his attitude precluding any such possibility. Mrs. Potter wondered if she had offended him—good Lord! was the young man that sensitive? She said, "Am I boring you, Mr. Carver?"

"I beg your pardon, ma'am!—I was thinking of something else. What did you say?"

"Oh, nothing that matters!"

Peevishly she relapsed in her own corner. Damn snobs! The people in this town were all alike—and she had thought him a rather nice young chap.

Neal brushed invisible cobwebs from his eyes. He had scarcely been aware that he was in an automobile, let alone of Mrs. Potter's presence or of what she was saying. Before him marched Owen's shoulders and brown neck, merging into a million other pairs of shoulders and a million other necks, a sea of brown and gold marching into the shimmer that was France. He faced Mrs. Potter.

"I'm awfully sorry, ma'am—I must tell you something—I want to quit my job!"

If he had announced that he wanted to get out and walk, she wouldn't have been more taken aback.

"Your job? Oh, yes! But you just got a raise!"

"Yes, I did. Please don't think I'm ungrateful, ma'am. It isn't because I'm dissatisfied. It's—it's something entirely different."

"I know." Mrs. Potter broke in with conviction that verged on enthusiasm. In a trice she became a new woman, as different from the prattler of a moment before as the sunburst from the shower. All her stilted sprightliness fell away before the genuine thing that had seized her mind. "I know—you don't have to tell me—Mr. Carver, you don't like the business! Isn't that it? Well, let me tell you something—I don't, either! I haven't liked it for a long time, a nigger business! I don't blame you. Now I'm going to tell you something confidential—something just between you and I—Mr. Carver, I'm changing the business, I'm branching out, I've got a scheme that will knock your eye out. Mr. Carver, do you use toothpaste?"

Bewildered, he answered, "Of course I do!"

"Nearly everybody does," agreed Mrs. Potter. She was glowing. "Toothpastes and mouthwashes are the biggest sellers in America. The public's wild about them. The public's been educated—people want to be nice—pretty—popular. I use two kinds of toothpaste myself, and I guess I've experimented with a thousand. How would you like to be in the toothpaste business, Mr. Carver? It's toney—aristocratic—and there's a fortune in it."

"Why, I never thought. I mightn't mind it at all. But honestly that isn't what I meant—"

"Never mind—I got what you meant as soon as you opened your mouth. You don't have to tell me about Whiteine; I know the way people talk. But they won't talk that way about Aseptiline! There—I've told you, Mr. Carver. That's my scheme—that's my new toothpaste—Aseptiline. Converted from a formula discovered by chemists in government laboratories. Listen—I've already got them working on it in the Chattanooga factory, and not a soul knows it—not even Rowlett. In another six months we'll put Aseptiline into every drug store in this country!"

Neal blinked in a kind of resentful torpor. Why in the world was she telling him all this? She had snatched his crisis from his burning heart and ridden off with it on a ridiculous hobby of her own, and he could do nothing but stare and say, "It sounds great, Mrs. Potter." Yearning to cry out his own hunger, he must listen instead to ravings about aristocratic mouthwash factories. Yet in those very ravings was something so vigorous that he kindled in spite of himself, the Potter ambitions towered above small personal affairs, and his wonder grew that a person capable of manipulating every drug store in the United States should choose him for a confidant.

Mrs. Potter's eyes shone like foxfire as she leaned toward her companion. No reason had animated her explosion. She, too, had been tortured in spirit, and to let out her secret to a Carver— to a country clubber, to one of those people—was somehow rejuvenating.

"How would you like a job with Aseptiline, Mr. Carver?"

"I don't want a job at all," blurted Neal; "I want to get in the war."

"The war?"

Mrs. Potter repeated the word slowly, without sneer or emphasis, as though she had never heard of war—of any war. And she looked at Neal with the same expressionless inquiry on her face. She had thought very little about the war—something that took up a lot of space in the newspapers, that did things both bothersome and splendid to business, and that, lately, had been getting under one's nose in a way one couldn't completely ignore. But even this Corinth war—the war of Liberty Loans and flags and speeches and bands and Uncle Sam cabbage instead of sauerkraut—even this war became part of the scenery and one got used to it and went on attending to business and going to Norma Talmadge movies and giving a dollar to the Red Cross and thinking. no more about the war. She hadn't known anyone who had gone to the war; the war really didn't have much to do with her.

Mrs. Potter had thought very little about Neal Carver, either. He was a nice-looking young man who happened to work for her, his existence given a slight importance because somebody had said he belonged to an old family. It had pleased her to have such a young man working for her, so she had impulsively raised his salary in one of those clairvoyant, something-to-be-gained-here moments which had inspired her before to her profit. But now this young man wanted to go to the war, and not only was he a young man who worked for her but who sat in her limousine with a strange passion in his nice- looking face. She no more understood the causes behind that passion than she did what going to the war meant, but she saw the young man in a handsome uniform with those other young men in front of Brundage's, she had a queer flashback to the fraternity boys she used to know—the one who gave her the pin and it turned out to be real emeralds—and the war and Neal Carver suddenly quivered alive. She put out her gloved hand and touched his arm.

"You really want to go?"

"I'd give anything to go," said Neal, huskily.

Genevieve leaned back. "Well, I guess I know how you feel. I never did pay much attention to history and patriotism and it seems to me we'd be better off to let those foreign countries alone when they get to squabbling. But I suppose all your friends are going and you'd feel sort of left out. What are you going to do— get into one of those officers' camps?"

"If I can."

"Well, I guess you can all right—with your friends."

"It isn't that," said Neal.

"What is it? Nothing the matter with you, is there?" asked the experienced Mrs. Potter.

"Oh, no, I'm fit enough. Better than a lot they're taking," he added bitterly, thinking of Jack Burr's eyes. He hesitated. "It's my people."

"Don't they want you to go?"

Uncle Gates denouncing the Huns, Berenice ablaze in her canteen uniform, his mother silently watching, always watching. ...

"I honestly don't know," said Neal. "It—isn't that."

He couldn't tell her what it was, he couldn't tell her they were poor. But Mrs. Potter, waiting for the explanation that did not come, guessed it.

"Well—" she covered awkwardly, and stopped.

A notion had occurred as arresting as her decision to save Mrs. Genelli and the Armenians. Compared to this young man, who made a hundred dollars a week and couldn't go to war because his family would miss it, she was fabulously rich. That was all that stood between him and being an officer—a hundred dollars a week—walking in with jingling spurs and the light flashing on gold braid—"Mrs. Genelli, I want you to meet Captain Carver!"—shucks, she could set him up to the war and never know the difference!

But better think twice; that money for Armenia hadn't got her much, had it?—besides, this was different; he wouldn't take it; too proud.

"Listen," said Mrs. Potter, "I don't want you to think I'm butting in, but if it's money that's worrying you, we've been talking it over at the office—about releasing some of the men for service, I mean—and it may be we could do something for you."

Bugles screamed wildly in the darkness, the blood thumped in Neal's temples.

He said hoarsely: "Look here, you don't think I brought this up—"

"My goodness, no! I guess I know a gentleman when I see one, Mister Carver!"

Mrs. Potter laughed. Her mind still danced ahead. "Mrs. Sims, meet Captain Carver—"

"Of course," she hedged, "we haven't done anything definite yet."

Neal laughed, too—sadly.

"It's mighty nice of you, mighty nice!—even to consider it. But it's out of the question, anyway. I couldn't accept anything like that."

"Why not? I guess I can have a soldier if I want to!"

She laughed again, as pleased with herself as Cora Potts in a new pink teddy. … "Certainly, Captain Carver! At the club tonight? I'd be charmed!

"You wait," she declared. "You wait and see. I guess Complexion Refineries is patriotic, all right."

CHAPTER TWELVE
WAR

RAISING MONEY by public subscription had become an American science in 1917. When the business men of Corinth essayed to find half a million dollars for the Red Cross, they set about it with no illusions as to the natural generosity of the human heart. A prosperous but penny-wise community must be excited, bewitched, shamed and frightened into "giving till it hurt," and to kick up exactly that kind of dust in the community's mind meant the mobilization of many forces and the unstinted spending of money to get money. Hence Mrs. Potter, drafted gladly into the service of her country, came to her job to discover it already fortified with ammunition sufficient to have elected a president. To this she added certain weapons of her own and a Napoleonic talent that startled the gentlemen who had chosen her primarily because there was nobody else to choose.

"We're missing a good bet," said Mrs. Potter to her assistant in the second week of the campaign. She rocked elegantly in a swivel chair in the office assigned to her at Red Cross headquarters. The glass top of her desk was buried in cards, letters, reports, buttons, printer's proofs. On the wall behind her, a map of Corinth adjoined a chart pimpled with different coloured tacks. Posters covered the other walls. Death strove with Valour, the Red Cross nurse mothered the world, and

Conscience cried: "What Are YOU Doing to Help?" Mrs. Potter, rocking elegantly, stared through the posters at her missed bet.

"They brought in the crew of that German ship yesterday," she said. "More than a hundred of them, and they're all out on the south side at that interment camp or whatever you call it. I tell you we're missing a bet in those sailor boys, Neal."

Mrs. Potter's assistant looked puzzled. He had stopped checking a list headed "Laundries and Dry Cleaners" and was turned around in his chair regarding his chief. Since their conversation in her automobile three weeks before, he had seen much of Mrs. Potter, and toward Mrs. Potter experienced a variety of reactions. When she had first carried him off from Complexion Refineries immediately on being notified of her new laurels, he had not known whether to be glad or sorry. The work was a relief from depigmented housemaids and rejoicing Pullman porters, but the woman was disconcerting. Then, as she swooped him through a fury of preparations, he got over his awe of Mrs. Potter; he found her young, almost innocent, where he had thought her puissance itself, and in those moments when she forgot poise before her assistant he preferred her to the mannered exquisite, he warmed to a sudden flash of slang, he began actually to like Mrs. Potter. Too busy for brooding in this storm of quotas and budgets and ballyhoo where dynamic Mrs. Potter coloured everything, he was almost happy. Only the posters, mutely interrogating his honour, he could never quite forget.

"I don't get you," he said. "Those Germans? They're enemy aliens. They'd be fighting against us if they were free. You don't think for a minute they're going to give to the Red Cross?"

"Why not?" It was astounding how Mrs. Potter brooked no impossibilities; it was she who had suggested coin boxes in the street cars, and, by George! the company had let her do it. "The Red Cross isn't a one-country proposition, is it? It's for

everybody—humanity! Like as not we'll save Germans and
Russians right along with our boys." Mrs. Potter was a little
vague as to which side was whose. "I'll bet if it was put up to those
sailors right, they'd come across. If they're broke, we'll advance
them the money. The important thing is to get them on the dot-
ted line and put it in the papers. You get the idea?—'If German
prisoners can give to your Red Cross, what about YOU?'—See?"

Neal chuckled. "By George, they might, at that. That's really
a great hunch!"

"Well, you see what you can do. Get a hold of your sister and
some of those other girls. Be sure and get pretty ones. Send them
out there this afternoon. I'm going to a luncheon. That church
bunch isn't on their toes like they ought to be, and I want to tell
'em what the niggers did down at Big Bethel."

Neal, alone, telephoned Berenice. As he waited for his number, he smiled grimly, anticipating what Berenice would say. "That
awful Mrs. Potter" had commandeered her social acquaintances
with painful ruthlessness, but there was "some'n about her" difficult to escape. Young ladies of Corinth were her special prey, they
formed majorities on all her committees, and once captured, the
craftiest found themselves going on distasteful missions and
fuming over card indices when they would much rather have
been riding and dancing with handsome young officers.

"Oh, dear, Neal! Some'n else? But I can't! I absolutely can't!"

It was no new wail. He had heard it scores of times, and usually it was only the prelude to surrender. It was extraordinary,
he thought, how, with all the moaning and scandalizing, they
did what Mrs. Potter asked them to do. The fact was that a sur-
prising condition was burgeoning around Mrs. Potter—she was
getting popular. Her popularity was confined almost entirely to
the younger set, to the pretty girls she had deliberately sought
out for her workers, and to their squires. They flocked around

her despite the demands she made on them; they might "run her down" among themselves but they liked going to her house. She had moved from her hotel and leased the old Cheney place; its latchstring was hospitably out to all callers, and here, among the Cheney portraits and her own paintings and statuary blandly dug out of storage, a rendezvous had developed for gay spirits. The pretty girls dropped by to report, the young officers trooped along, for the frost was eternal on Mrs. Potter's juleps, and when the day's work was over, who cared if campaigning gave way to frolic, if the rugs were kicked back, the victrola turned on and the cocktails and the shimmy shaken? Certainly not young Mrs. Potter. As she said, she always had a houseful of people before coming to Corinth and she just loved entertaining again.

"Oh, Neal, have I *got* to?" wept Berenice. "Well, all right! But I hope Gen Potter breaks her neck!"

Neal returned to his laundries and dry cleaners. Each name on his list must be looked up in a file index of subscriptions received, and the goats separated from the sheep. Another list must then be made so that every goat in twenty-four hours would receive a special delivery appeal. If this was unavailing, his name went on a third list headed "Assignments for Moppers Up," and here Mrs. Potter's young ladies took the warpath. Results so far had justified her belief in them and in the Potter system of intensified patriotism.

While Neal thumbed the cards and ran his pencil through the patriots' names, his thoughts travelled like two motor cars. One chugged along the main road, functioning perfectly from laundry to laundry; at the same time, the other roved all sorts of alien highways and byways. Calculating the sum the Star Laundry ought to pay if the Excelsior Laundry gave two hundred dollars, he wondered what Mrs. Potter's husband had been like and how old she was when he died. He finished the laundry list and took up druggists while, in the second car, he discussed with Uncle Gates the righteousness of work. But presently there was a collision, a complete smashup in front of Jolo's Pharmacy, as it were, and Neal, tapping with his pencil, let one car whirl him.

Across the room, Miss Conners surreptitiously read "The Genius" behind a pile of newspapers. Above him, for sixteen floors, men worked in shirtsleeves and stenographers mused on beaches and odorono while they typed—a dentist on the fourth floor split a tooth, a blonde cried in a loan shark's office, in Room 940 two clerks threw dice for nickels; above all that, the sun blazed. Outside, where people sweltered on their engrossing affairs, streets smelled hot and gaseous. In a hundred camps drill sergeants shouted at the lean ranks, and somewhere in Flanders half a body swayed grotesquely on the wire. Neal's pencil point broke in his fingers. This day three months, perhaps, Owen would be on the Atlantic.

"What Are YOU Doing to Help?" the silent posters taunted, and he could only whisper, "What?" … Laundries, druggists, grocers, butchers, dictation to Miss Conners, adding machines, fretful women, printers, haggling over discounts—"it's for the Red Cross, you know; it's for our boys." … Our boys! If he were but crippled, white-haired, anything to conceal his own young manhood! … What gallant performance to write, "Dear sir, we know you have deferred sending in your subscription simply because you have overlooked this opportunity, etc., etc.!" Why not with equal justice, "Dear Mr. Carver, we know you have deferred sending in your enlistment simply because" … because he was a coward! Because it was cowardice, nothing else, not to find a way out of this backwater. … Surely there was a way! Mrs. Potter had opened one, once, and he had drawn back, proud, sensitive. How he regretted his pride!—longed for the opportunity again, wondered if she had forgotten, and still was too proud to approach her. For Mrs. Potter said nothing, Mrs. Potter had rushed him off his feet with her Red Cross just as she had with her toothpaste. Mrs. Potter probably thought, if she thought about it at all, that he was glad to be in "war work," even war work concerned chiefly with egging young girls onto imprisoned sailors. Well, he wasn't—he was damn sick of it—yet he did nothing, he *could* do nothing! ... "What Are YOU Doing to Help?" ...

Meanwhile Mrs. Potter had attended her luncheon, had mendaciously announced that the coloured Christians were outgiving the white, had appealed to the latter not to forget Florence Nightingale and Clara Barton (whom she herself had never heard of until the week before), and after sundry other references to God, "Corinth spirit" and the Huns, stepped again into her motor and ordered Josef to drive to the Nickajack Building.

The car moved south along Cherokee Avenue, and Mrs. Potter gazed out at Corinth. Other motors moved with hers, people walked slowly in the sunshine, block by block the traffic and the sidewalk crowds grew thicker. Here and there, as the shining grey monster passed, heads turned and hats were lifted. An old gentleman emerging from a bank stopped abruptly and bowed from the waist. A woman in another car waved, leaning out to be sure that she was seen. In front of Brundage's there was considerable stir—heads went bare all along the line of gallants and slim hands fluttered like a covey of risen partridges. Mrs. Potter smiled and nodded. She wondered who many of them were.

So Curtis Rowlett, writing in a small black book in his private office, was surprised by a visitor who did not knock.

Hastily he rumpled papers over his work, jumped to his feet and welcomed her explosively.

"Well—stranger! How's the campaign?"

She did not like it—she did not like it at all! this unusual effusiveness from her Vice-President. And she saw that he was nervous yet there was something unabashed in the look he gave her, and altogether, as she sat down, she was put about and suddenly suspicious and quite ruffled out of the complacency she had been enjoying only a few moments before. She had come there on a matter of some importance, she had intended to take him into her confidence, to broach her plans for Aseptiline, for more and more she was feeling the need to "get out of this nigger business." But almost instantly resentment and distrust silenced her, for as she studied Curtis, taking in his clothes and his grin and the air with which he straddled his chair, the thought stabbed her that here, in the person of this sallow, undersized young turkeycock, with his monogrammed shirt and his dirty fingers, was the marplot of her destiny, the only one among all the men and women surrounding the rich Mrs. Potter who could leer through her splendid armour and let her realize without a spoken word the thing he saw. And for the first time in their years of understanding the thought dismayed her.

She attacked on an irrelevant issue. "The campaign's swell— no thanks to you. How the hell do you expect me to raise money when my own employees loaf like a lot of dirty tramps? I put you on a committee to get publicity—flags, fireworks, pep!—and you get it by manicuring your nails in the office all afternoon!

"God knows they need it," she added viciously.

"Oh, have a heart—"

Vainly he protested the necessity of attending to business. Vainly he pleaded that he had just come in, vainly pointed out results achieved, cards in the windows, columns in the newspapers, red crosses everywhere—Mrs. Potter was not appeased. She sat glowering through his expostulations and then let him have it. Curtis was a liar as well as a good-for-nothing loafer. Curtis slacked on the business like he did on everything. She was sick to death of his laziness and excuses.

Why, for two bits she'd close the office tomorrow and let him whistle for a living!

He listened with lips twisted into the semblance of the sneer he did not dare display, and he hated her through every fibre. He could not know that she lashed him merely because he reminded her of so much she wanted forgotten, that a sense of vulnerability caused her to strike where she was weakest to defend. Could he have penetrated to the motives behind her temper, he would have crowed instead of writhing.

Mrs. Potter got up. She felt better, but not much. After many days away from the office, after new faces and new talk, after the homage and the triumphs and the intoxications of power, the very presence of Curtis was unendurable. And she had planned to let this worm in on Aseptiline! As she slammed the door, she wished never so heartily that Whiteine was buried along with The Mansion and Duke Tedder, and Curtis Rowlett in the deepest grave under them all.

She did not stop at Red Cross headquarters, but went home and into the tub. At five o'clock, when Berenice Carver dashed in at the head of a noisy company, she found her presiding over felicity with her wonted charm.

Lights sparkled, laughter echoed from the wainscot of the immense room where the Cheneys looked down from their frames on the younger generation. Two young officers clinked highballs before the Carrara mantel. Regis Marr, whose mother had been a Cheney, spanked out the "Darktown Strutters Ball" on the piano while a major and a training-camp protégé swapped limericks across her bob. From beyond the windows, open to the twilight, more laughter and the aroma of honeysuckle rose from the Cheney garden.

Berenice stood on the threshold and screamed.

"Gen Pottah! Gen Pottah! You come heah this minute!"

The new mistress of the old Cheney place-turned from the wall where she had been telling that gay bachelor, Clark Burton, how, as a little girl, she always thought the etching of Notre Dame was Westminster Abbey. Graciously she moved away from memories of childhood to surrender to the fluff and outcry that immersed her half-way across the room. Eight girls charged her, all talking at once, a medley out of which issued the one clear fact that something dreadful had happened.

"For the love of heaven, girls, hush up and let one of you talk!"

"You tell her, Berenice—"

"Well, we went out to that crazy old camp and at first they weren't goin' to let us see a soul, but Nancy Ann knew the Colonel, she went to school with his daughter at Sweetbriar, and she vamped him, and he was a nice old thing—"

"I did not!"

"You did so! And anyway, we wouldn't have got in at all if it hadn't been for a cute sergeant; but we did, and the Colonel said all right, he'd let us talk to their head man—the Germans', I mean, he was a commander Bruckner or Breekner or something like that, and he's a real Count! Well, the Colonel got him in and he was tall and handsome in a Prussian kind of way—you know! and he had a little blond moustache and he made the most beautiful bow and he spoke beautiful English! At first he was very nice, but as soon as he found out what we wanted, he froze right up. He stood like a ramrod for a minute and then he said to the Colonel, 'Sir, may I express myself to these young women?'—yes'm, he said women! I reckon the Colonel didn't know what was comin', because he said, 'Certainly,' and you bet your life we didn't know, we were all smilin' and just ready to eat him up, he was so cute, when he cut lopse and gave us down in the country! It wasn't so much what he said, but the way he said it, kind of crunchin' his

words and spittin' them at us, and he said certainly not, he would
not allow us to see his men if permission depended on him—they
were prisoners and must bow to the will of their jailors—but if
he understood us cor'ectly, we were askin' them to give their last
money to succor and comfort the soldiers of an enemy nation
when their own soldiers were fightin' and dyin' and their own
families starvin' to death—oh, and a lot more like that!—and
then he clipped us short and saluted the Colonel and said, 'Sir,
have I made myself clear?' and the Colonel was red as fire and he
gruffed out, 'You have, sir!—I shall respect your wishes!' and out
the Count went, and out we went, and I'll declare to goodness, I
never was so ashamed in my life!"

Berenice spent her last breath on a silent room. The major at
the piano avoided his companion's eye. The two young officers by
the mantel exchanged a glance and looked away as though each
had caught the other at dirty work. Only Clark Burton drawled,
"Why, the nervy scoundrel!" The girls all watched Mrs. Potter,
breathlessly, like children waiting for the rabbit to pop out of the
hat. And Mrs. Potter, after one angry shake of her shoulders, did
not disappoint them.

"Pshaw!" she said, "I wouldn't get all steamed up about it.
We weren't going to get any real money out of them, anyway. It
would have made a good story for the papers—that's all. Well,
it's a better story like it is. Neal—call up and give it to them. You
know where the 'phone is. They ought to put it on the front page."

Mrs. Potter's assistant, who had arrived with his workers to
take counsel on the failure, looked uncertain.

"Why, they wouldn't want that," he said.

"And you were a newspaper man!" Mrs. Potter's smile was
not unkindly. "Listen, honey, this is the best piece of propaganda
we've dug out of this campaign yet. Don't you see?—'German
Sailors Insult Corinth Girls—Red Cross Workers Sneered at by

Hun Count'—it's good for an advertisement! Phone Mr. Corson and ask him—Where 'Do YOU Belong, on the Red Cross honour roll or in a prison camp with those who won't give?' "

"But he really didn't insult us!" cried Nancy Ann Morgan. "He was real sweet!"

Mrs. Potter put an arm around her.

"Nancy Ann, you're a child. The man meant to insult you. Anyway, he's a German. Come on—you can have a cocktail if you won't tell Mother."

Neal hesitated by the door as fluff swirled with Mrs. Potter to the serving table. Something agonized and bitter rose to his lips. It was a good story, Mrs. Potter was right—but what a distortion, what a farce! What a mission for him, errand boy to the Red Cross, spreading lies about brave men. ... He stared, unseeing, with a captive's face.

Mrs. Potter saw it past the other gay faces, and a little frown settled in the pale blue eyes. She handed the shaker to Clark Burton.

"Well, Neal?" she asked as she came up to him. "Aren't you going to 'phone?"

He shook his head miserably. All the others were fixed on their own amusement.

"I can't do that," he said. "I can't do it!"

Looking at him, she said nothing. She was remembering the boy who sat at her side and told her he wanted to go to war, and to the intent expression that always rested in her gaze was added something else—a sudden pity.

Mrs. Potter did what for her was a curious thing. She took Neal's hand and held it between both of hers.

"That's all right, honey," she said. "We'll pass it up."

CHAPTER THIRTEEN
RALLY

THE AUDITORIUM of Corinth, future Half Million City. Largest municipal edifice south of Pittsburgh. Pride of all citizens, scene of all civic jubilees. Opera, prize fights, bicycle races, baby shows, horse shows, auto shows, dog shows. Shrine balls, Elks' balls, Red Men's balls, Odd Fellows' balls, Pan-Hellenic balls, conventions, revivals, cooking schools, track meets, concerts, graduations, dinners, debates, festivals, pageants, funerals, all held under this roof.

The auditorium, hub of what's going on in Corinth—and tonight packed to its ten thousand capacity, to the last bench against the rows of standees, to the last chair in the boxes suffocating with the brilliant and the great, to the farthermost tier of galleries lost under the steel beams, packed with sea and circle and wall of faces, pale fields and banks of faces sweating under the lights and the flags, flags, flags billowed wherever no faces show, flags of all nations but Germany and her allies; a single Old Glory cut by a monster Red Cross spanning the breadth of the stage, and beneath it another halfmoon of faces, and these, like the others, all pointed toward the man standing in the cup of the halfmoon, a small man in a white linen suit with a white mane of hair brushed up from his forehead, his gesturing arms taut, and his voice, a deep bell of a voice for so small a man, detonating into the glare and the heat and the hush of those listening ten thousands—

"... France—bled white! England! Desperately fighting with her back to the Channel while the blood of innocents waters the streets of London! What day will hear the thunder of Big Bertha in our own streets? See our skies black with enemy planes? We are not safe tonight from invasion! What instant may not bring the same hellish hordes that overwhelmed poor little Belgium—legions of the Beast!—bombarding our cities, laying waste our fields with fire and sword, ravishing our women, murdering our babes in the cradle. ... The Hun! ..."

The faces are immovable. But here and there a fan waves, feet shuffle, a chair creaks, and through ten thousand brains dart tremendous little thoughts that have nothing to do with death and rapine and tortured Belgium and the world at war.

Thinks Uncle Gates Carver, cautiously scratching his most grievous itches: "Ought to put cushions on these benches. Told 'em so! Told Peter Block they ought to have cushions like the old opera house. What good is it telling anybody anything in this town? Not like the old days. ... Bryan's speech. Torchlights, red fire, wine—what nights! We cut loose then, we got mad, we—felt things. Wild young bucks. Nowadays it's the women. ... Neal's a good boy, but he doesn't feel the war. Wonder why he wouldn't come tonight? ... This is no way to raise money, one big meeting! They won't give. Too hot here, benches too hard. ... What'll I give? Got to give something. Wouldn't do not to. What's she got in her purse? If she'd slip me something. ... A little loan. ..."

Thinks Mrs. Carver, clasping her quiet hands: "He's going ... going and nothing can stop him, nothing can help. ... Nothing. ... He's going to war. ... Cannon and shells, the blood, all the horrible blood. ... My little boy, my Neal, flesh of my flesh. ... My flesh, his flesh ... burned, suffering. ... He's going. ..."

Thinks Jim Corson, from his place six feet behind the speaker: "Won't he ever stop? Won't he ever get through? In this heat—I told him to make it short! Old fool! Damned old fool! There he goes again—'They shall not pass!'—if he's said it once, he's said it fifty times. Ten minutes more and this crowd will walk out on us. Lord, what a chance! Twelve thousand people out there, a hundred thousand dollars if we once get 'em going. There's Tom Wentworth. If he gives a thousand, Brick Ely'll give five. Where's Freddy? Great Peter, where's Freddy? If he forgets that Central Bank subscription. ... And those others. ... Lord, Lord! Why doesn't he stop? They're fidgeting, you can see it. Fagged out. Another ten minutes and it will be too late for Mrs. Potter—oh, Lord, strike him dead! ..."

Thinks Mrs. Werner Sims, her lorgnette repelling base humanity: "I ought to be up there. Why didn't she put me on her committee? I'll never forgive her—never! I don't see her. Why isn't she up there? Funny—I don't see the others, either. Helen said they were going to wear costumes. She'll make them ridiculous! ... I hope she does. I hope she makes a fool of herself ... A total stranger. ... What do they know about her? ... Money. ... If Werner only had money. ..."

Thinks Curtis Rowlett, peering over shoulders that jam an exit: "Well, the old buzzard certainly got her crowd, but if she don't move quick, they're lost. Old Windbags is gassing them to death—and heavy dough in there, too. Look at 'em—old man Ely, and Tom Wentworth, and Colonel Sartain, and Tracy Tennyson—Keerist! Those boxes are filthy with jack. But they won't loosen up unless she shoots pretty soon, not the way they're already drifting out, there in the back. Shucks, it'll take a bombshell to wake that crowd. ... Well, she's got it if she'll only shoot. A cute little idea, and what credit do I get for it? ... Wonder if Thelma remembers those crazy dames in Peachburg? Wonder if she remembers that night? And that fool preacher! Didn't bat an eye when I give her the tip. But you can't tell about Thelma any more, what she thinks, what she remembers. You can't tell nothin' about her. ..."

Thinks Berenice Carver, trembling on one foot in the line outside the big double doors: "Oh, why don't we move? Why don't we move? We've been here hours—and I'm melting—and I know my nose is shiny—I can feel it shiny! And the perspiration soaking through! Does it show? Oh, damn, if the red cross runs! It'll ruin everything—everything! And I looked so nice! Why doesn't Mrs. Potter do something? Heaven knows, she's done enough! But why doesn't she do something *now*? Why don't we move? Why don't we move? ..."

And then, behind her, the electric voice: "Now, girls—"

As the Honourable Judah Pettigrew's arms sank from supplication to the Allies' god and the long silence assured even the hopeless that this time he was, indeed, through, the auditorium of Corinth expelled a mighty sigh. The Honourable Judah accepted it for emotion, a tribute sweeter than the applause that followed, but Jim Corson knew it for what it was—the stretch before the bolt—and in an instant he was at Pettigrew's side, one hand braced against the gathering cheers.

"Ladies and gentlemen—"

He never finished. Somewhere behind the heat and glare a whistle piped, double doors swung back, a thunderblast of trumpets struck the unexpecting thousands. The effect was galvanic—an incendiary needle driven into a nodding giant. A hundred men sprang up. Women squealed. In the fourth row, Uncle Gates Carver rose with the others, gobbling across his neighbours' heads. If the entire German army was at the portcullis, he defied them to come on.

But there was no one—nothing—only the long, strident blast clamouring over the empty portals, reverberating across the

startled rows. Even Jim Corson, stunned to forgetfulness, gaped
at the doors in wonder at what they would precipitate.

Then, with the trumpets, crashed the drums, fifes screamed
like a thousand valkyries, a flash of light ricocheted from a baton's
tip, and overpowering unison erupted on the auditorium—

> "Over there! Over there!
> Send the word—send the word—
> Over there! …"

Down the aisle they came, the bands of Corinth, not one, not
two, but all—Shrine band, Elks' band, Firemen's Drum Corps,
Corinth Cadet band, National Guard band, Knights of Pythias
band, Boy Scout band, band of the Turnverein gone over bodily
to the Corinth Home Guard, a dozen bands in one, a score of
instruments swelled to twelve score, and the multiplied drums
and fifes and horns and trumpets tuned to one pitch, hammered
to one time, pounding away at one strain—

> "Send the word—send the word—
> Over there!"

One man led them, stumping a few paces in advance of the
Shriners' zouave trousers and red fezes. He was no ordinary
drum major in glitter of braid and plunging shako, he was a runt
in drab yellow, a brimless cap scarcely covered his head, his baton
was not a baton, but a crutch, and when he waved it, there was
none who could not see that his left leg was gone at the knee. The
little man hopped rather than strutted toward the platform. Yet
he went fast, and the Shriners' zouave trousers, the purple jackets
of the Elks, the red shirts of firemen, the gay cadet uniforms, all
the colours that surged with the music as it shook the floor and

puffed the flags, did not capture the eye like the drab yellow of that one little man, hopping fast and waving his crutch.

Old ladies in the boxes near the entrance had put their fingers to their ears when the trumpets clapped. Deserters outside the building had halted and turned back. Blocks away, with the roll of drums, small boys had whooped and legged it for the auditorium. And now, as the first band reached the platform and the last was yet to stream through the doors, the roar of the audience drowned the bands themselves. People suddenly were impelled to abandon. They stood on benches, handkerchiefs tossed in a white frenzy, the cheering was continuous, like that at a football game with a touchdown imminent. At the foot of the platform, citizens seized the little soldier, lifted him and pushed him to where other hands took hold—he slid from shoulder to shoulder, grinning uneasily.

"We'll be ooo-ver!" boomed the drums. "We're coming ooo-ver!" sang the trumpets, and into the Corinth auditorium, through the double doors on the drummers' heels, marched incarnate glory. These were women. These were girls. But they were women and girls of an anointed order, heiresses to a legend so hallowed that, however mean or cruel they were individually, as a class they were saints, and whatever share of cruelty and meanness they had suffered individually from men, as members of the immaculate host they received only man's worship. The women of the South! The young girls, as well as the others, women of the Old South; of the tradition of purity and chivalry and easy death for a smile and a rose, and marching now as one woman, herself a heroine sublime, the Red Cross Nurse. They were dressed alike in white skirts and white blouses, a white cap on every head and a red cross on every breast. They carried nothing and they did not march well, some walking too rapidly and others jostling in the narrow aisle, but they marched with heads up and crosses spilled like blood against the whiteness, and they sang the song the bands played, "Over there! Over there! ..."

"They don't sing as well as them Philatheas did," thought Curtis Rowlett.

The auditorium went mad.

Many minutes after the last straggler had climbed the platform and arranged herself as part of the tableau of beauty and patriotism crowded under Old Glory, many minutes after the drums were silent and the last fifer no longer puckered his tired lips, Jim Corson still stood with a hand on the one-legged boy's shoulder, waiting for bedlam to die. He had no doubts now—he himself was too shaken for doubts—but they must at least hear him before the money could flow.

"Ladies and gentlemen"—no moment, this, for a speech— "who'll give to the Red Cross?"

They chalked the figures on the big blackboard where already four hundred thousand showed, Andy Johnson on a stepladder, three computers below, and Jim Corson yelling through a megaphone as the canvassers scurried to the platform with the filled-in forms. ...

"Central Bank of Corinth, five thousand dollars! ... Sunny South Bakeries, three thousand dollars! ... Tri-State Knitting Mills, five thousand dollars. ... Tennyson Candy Company, TEN THOUSAND DOLLARS!" ...

These were the big ones, most of them hooked days before and held back for the stampede. Start high. Hush those fives and tens. Make 'em ashamed to give a dollar. Make 'em give till it hurts. Send the women down. Send the pretty girls. Sign 'em up! Knock 'em down! ...

"Five thousand dollars from S. J. Sartain on condition we get another five thousand. Who'll match five thousand with five thousand? Who'll give five thousand to get ten? 'Attaboy! Five thousand dollars—"

Watch those exits. Get a girl at that exit. Don't let 'em hesitate. Hit 'em while they're hot. Blanks! We're running out of *blanks!* More BLANKS! ...

"Come on, Corinth! Let's go over the top, Corinth! Over the top tonight! We're going o-ver, we're going cover!"

... Better shoot some little ones. Don't let the little fellows get away. Give 'em those kid subscriptions. ...

"And the kiddies, too!"

... Give 'em Savings of a Soldier's Mother. Give 'em the school pledges. Give 'em the fraternal order pledges. ...

"Benevolent and Protective Order of Elks—Ancient Order of Red Men—Corinth Orphans' Home!—Corinth OLD LADIES' HOME!"

"I don't blame you for cheering, folks! When the poor and unfortunate, the indigent and helpless—"

... What's the total now? Tell that band to play again. Tell 'em to march up the aisle and back when I announce this one. Tell 'em to play "Over There." ...

"Over there! ... Over there! Send the word—send the word— over there! ... Well be oover—! We're coming oo-ver! ... And we won't—come—back—till it's over—over—there!" ...

Jubilee in the Corinth auditorium. Tumult where the dogs barked and the Shriners danced. Ten thousand are going over the top for city, country and humanity. A woman, weeping, shuts the empty purse. "Here, sir!" shouts an old man. No satisfaction for Mrs. Werner Sims to raise her lorgnette now. The thing is there, in black and white, in dollars and cents, in the crowd's roar, in the bellow from Jim Corson's megaphone. And while Berenice Carver powders her nose and Curtis Rowlett sneers, Corinth goes over—over the top—and Mrs. Genevieve Potter, challenging the flashlights between the one-legged soldier and the Honourable Judah Pettigrew, assures the press of her gratitude for the victory won this night by the women of the South, the Old South, of whom—need they ask?—Mrs. Potter was proud to be the leader.

The room was dark. A hot, close night, with the cicadas droning endlessly out there in the garden.

No other sound. Then, as fingers groped for the electric switch, something stirred by the couch.

Mrs. Potter gave a nervous gasp, and sent light blazing.

"Neal!" she cried. "Good God—how you scared me!"

She laughed, crossing the room and throwing her wrap on the piano.

"What on earth are you doing here? Why didn't you come to the rally? It was grand! When those bands began to play—"

She saw that he was drunk.

He stood where he had risen, his hair roughed and his body swaying as he blinked at her. There was a decanter on the table and on the floor at his feet was a glass half full of whisky. He must have been lying there in the dark, drinking, until he fell asleep.

Suddenly he began to sing.

"When the ba-a-nd begins to play, ti-um-ti-ah, ti-um- ti-ay!"

He beat time, snapping his fingers.

"When the ba-a-nd—hey, Mrs. Potter, let's have a drink!"

She was not shocked—the young officers, even the young ladies, often grew hilarious at Mrs. Potter's—but she was surprised. If one leads the women of the Old South, one does not expect to discover a young man in intoxicated possession of one's couch at midnight. The butler must have let him in. And that was all right, the butler knew Mr. Carver, and though he might have been there for hours and no telling how much he had had—why not? It was just Neal, unexpectedly but rather engagingly drunk. Better to humour him. She needed a bracer, she was dog tired.

"Sure—I'll have a drink!"

Just the same, she was glad she was alone. Suppose she had asked Berenice and her family to stop instead of sending them on in the car? Mrs. Carver wouldn't have understood at all.

"Here's how, Neal."

"Happy days!"

The glass wavered in his hand, whisky slopped down the front of his coat, and she wiped it away with her handkerchief.

"Sorry. ... Awful lot of bother. But I been celebratin'. Celebratin' all by myself. ... Glorious Red Cross victory!"

Again the glass flourished.

"Hooray! Hooray for America! Hooray for all the little soldier boys! All goin' away to war!"

Mrs. Potter put her arm around him.

"Sit down, Neal. Sit down here. What's the matter, honey?"

Still with her arm around him, he stared at nothing with a grin on his face, and all at once it broke up, his face seemed to come unbuttoned with emotions tearing and spurting through the skin, and Mrs. Potter did not have to be subtle or unduly sympathetic to know that he cried because he was wretchedly unhappy.

"Don't mind, Neal honey," she said. "You're all in."

He would straighten up in a minute, he would jerk away from her caress. And he would be ashamed; drunk as he was, he would despise himself for going to pieces that way. Well, she was truly sorry for the poor kid, she had gotten kind of fond of him, as fond as she was of anybody, and she'd seen this business coming on. The damn war, she supposed. It was a shame he was tied down to his family. If she had her way—"Shucks!" she thought, as once before, "I can set him up to the war!"

"Don't mind, Neal," she repeated, and her arm tightened. "Come on—I want another drink. Won't you pour me a drink, honey?"

That would straighten him all right; that would give him a chance to pull himself together. Mumbling apology, he got up, and while he refilled the glasses she glanced across at the mirror, and fixed the loosening straps of her gown, and, when he turned, was leaning back, one hand behind her head, and was smiling up at him.

"All right, buddy? Let's forget! I'm all in, too. ..."

She was all in—dog tired she was. The rally tonight. And all these weeks of fussing and fuming and bossing other people, fighting the women and pretending all the time you liked them. Lord, Lord! How she'd love to be herself just once—let down and be yourself and like somebody for liking's sake and have them like you!

"Sit down, Neal. I'm not going to bite you."

But he remained standing, staring at her. What had he been doing? Crying? What a baby! And in front of a good sport like Mrs. Potter. ... A good sport like Mrs. Potter. He saw her, relaxed and smiling, through a bright mist. Relaxed on the couch, and the bright mist on her gown and the bare shoulders rising out of it and her bare arm curving behind her head. The bright mist was even a part of her smiling bright eyes. He sat down.

"Here's how, Neal!"

"Happy days. ..."

She was close to him, as close as the hot, close night. There was silence, only the cicadas droning out there in the garden, and then a little sigh rose with the perfume from the shoulder near Neal's burning eyes.

"Neal ... Put out the light, honey!"

So the Cheney portraits were spared the spectacle of a Joan of the Old South forgetting her dignity.

CHAPTER FOURTEEN
BLACKMAIL

THROUGH that fevered summer, as June wilted into July and August's sun began to scorch the new pine cities springing up on coast and midland, America moved complexly toward the war. On July twentieth a groping hand fished a capsule from a bowl in Washington; wires flashed "258" to millions waiting the numbers of the selective draft. Six days later the first American troops landed at a port in France. September saw thirty thousand conscripts under khaki. Over Texas an airplane did the Immerman turn, in New York the "Rainbow Division" paraded before the Secretary of War, and in Georgia an engineering camp hummed one day and the next was barren of life.

At about the same time, readers of the Saturday Evening Post observed a new advertisement, and a Senator in the smoking-room of the Congressional Limited recommended to a member of the French High Commission the dentifrice, "Aseptiline."

Before that, Neal Carver had passed his tests and was a member of the Second Officers' Training Camp.

Twilight was long over, but heat still soaked the camp like steam squeezed from a huge mop. Heat vapoured from the wet boards of the newly built barracks and rose in the darkness from the mud of the company street. The night smelled oppressively of kitchens and laundries, with a sickish sweet odour of disinfectant pervading everything. Neal, sprawled on his cot, reading his letters, felt the heat stick on the back of his neck and throb in his chafed feet. He was deadly weary, but it did not matter; he was where he had yearned to be.

"My own son," wrote Mrs. Carver, "we are all thinking of you and praying for you. It seems years since you went away, though I know it is only a few weeks. We miss you so, dear boy, and while we are all quite well here, I am counting the days till you get your first leave. Too bad you chose the infantry instead of the artillery. Then you might have been out at the fort where we could see you often. ... There is not much news here. ..."

He read on, automatically absorbing the gossip of family and town, while all the time his brain harried the problem conjured by the other letter at his elbow, the three lines in round, childish script penned on the monogrammed card. They might mean nothing, they might conceal matters trivial or joyous, yet he could not escape that other possibility, the crushing, incredible possibility that became less incredible, more crushing with every second he scoffed at it. A name in his mother's letter leaped out. ...

"Your sister is seeing a great deal of Mrs. Potter. Of course, I am very grateful to her for making it easier for you to enlist, and I am sure everyone in Corinth appreciates her splendid war work. (She is helping to organize the next Liberty Loan drive, by the way.) Yet I can't help having a queer feeling about her, that she is—what shall I say?—not a happy influence on the young people. After all, she is so much older, isn't she? Berenice laughs at me and says I am old-fashioned—she 'adores' Mrs. Potter— but I really wish you would speak to her when you come home. Berenice, I mean. I do not wish to be unjust, but I have this queer feeling that Mrs. Potter is a little fast."

Neal smiled grimly, then frowned. He experienced a gust of resentment toward his mother. Why should she always be so suspicious? Really, if it wasn't for Mrs. Potter, the family would be starving to death. ... And yet ... and yet ... women were uncanny! His mother's eyes, watching, fearful ... She had written that letter about Berenice, but she had aimed it at him. "So much older, isn't she?" Oh, yes, she had aimed it at him. ...

He rolled on his back, under the electric glare, and against his orange lids the events and the reactions of that night vividly shaped themselves.

He hadn't been ashamed. Only sick and confused at first, and, then, as memory clicked, stupidly amazed that it had happened. He had gotten quickly out of the strange bed, found a door opening into a bathroom, towels and a dressing gown there. The cold shower had picked him up, and though his head ached dully, he had answered with a calm voice when the knock came at the door. Mrs. Potter had entered with a tray ... the savour of hot coffee ... her arms fresh and smooth out of silken sleeves. ... She had smiled. ...

Later, "You mustn't act blue, Neal," she had said. "Are you remorseful? Listen, I made up my mind a long time ago never to regret anything that's over and done. Maybe we were silly, but I'm not sorry, honey. Sex is a funny thing; it's like all the rest of our senses, I reckon. You get hungry and you eat and nobody cares. Well, I guess I've been kind of starved for affection. ...

"And don't worry about the servants," she had added practically. "I told 'em you got stewed and I just put you to bed."

A good sport, Mrs. Potter. And he had liked her, after all.

That morning he was very grateful for the unconcern in her good-bye kiss. He was even more grateful for the "way she had taken it" a few mornings thereafter, when Mr. Rowlett announced in his surly way that the company would pay half the salary of men who entered service. That was Mrs. Potter's doing, but she didn't make a fellow feel under obligations. It never occurred to him that Mrs. Potter might have been fearful over his continued presence in Corinth; he had simply been wildly happy ... If it wasn't for that monogrammed card, unescapable under his right hand. ...

"Neal honey—"

As though she spoke to him—

"Something's happened. I've got to see you. Can't you get away for a few days? Wire me and I'll have Josef meet the train. Genevieve."

That was all.

But Neal, who was neither prude nor rake, merely a young man with appetites and a sense of honour, heard behind that appeal the rush of wings dark with the menace of an ancient code.

"You dirty little heel," said Mrs. Potter, quietly.

Curtis Rowlett cowered, defiant.

"You can't do that to me," he mumbled. "You can't do that to me."

"Who says I can't? Business is business. The outfit's sold—lock, stock and barrel. If your new boss don't want you, that's your hard luck. Don't come whining and blustering to me to save your job."

Despite herself, she felt a little sorry for him, he had gone so suddenly and disgustingly to pieces.

"What are you crying about, anyway, Curtis? You act like somebody had stolen your last nickel. You've had a pretty good thing out of this for the last few years—why, you must be worth twenty or thirty thousand! and that's a lot of money for a young fellow. Besides, you don't know yet but what this new bunch will keep you."

"Look here," he said, getting out of his chair and ramming his hands in his pockets with something of his old swagger. "Look here—I said you can't do this to me, and you can't! Who furnished the formula that started this business? I did! I own that formula and you damn well can't sell out without I give you the legal right!"

Mrs. Potter laughed aloud.

"Legal right! Sonny, you're not nearly as smart as you think you are. You know as well as I do that the formula you're talking about has as much to do with making Whiteine as milk has with whisky. The formulas used by Complexion Refineries, the formulas that go with this sale, are protected in my name, not yours. My lawyers saw to that years ago. And just to make sure, your last contract as Vice-President had a clause renouncing all claims to any patents, titles or proprietary rights whatever. You didn't read that contract very carefully, did you, Curtis? Too tickled over the raise to twenty thousand a year!"

He gaped at her, genuinely shocked. Not the least stupefying blow was the revelation of his own gullibility where he had always believed he had outsmarted a smart one. She had him—skinned, gutted, dried.

"Don't take it so hard, Curtis. Business is business. After all, it was me put up the money, wasn't it? If you'd hoed the row alone, you'd still be a twenty-dollar-a-week reporter in Peachburg."

Mrs. Potter leaned back, easy mistress of this or any situation in her own home.

"I didn't ask you out here to make a scene," she said. "I tell you you've been lucky. But the way you act, anybody'd think I'd accused you of robbing the till. I've simply sold the business—and that's that."

She was getting tired of this; the Vice-President of a nigger medicine company had taken up about enough of her evening; in a few more minutes she would show him the door.

Curtis had made no answer to her last remark, but glanced at her quickly and now took out a handkerchief and was dabbing at his lips, making a queer licking sound. He spoke slowly.

"You said—the deal—hadn't gone through? You said they—would be coming in—"

"The first of the month," said Mrs. Potter. "As soon as their audit confirms my estimate. You'll hear from them in a few days probably; their men will be in to see you next week, I imagine. But you don't have to bother about that; just give 'em anything they want. I'll introduce you to Thomas tomorrow. He's the man you want to impress. And I'll speak a word for you, Curtis. I want to see you get a good break."

He put up his handkerchief.

"Well, that's all right," he said huskily. "That's mighty good of you, Thelma.".

She let the old name slide by without a murmur—it had come out so palpably without intent, an unthinking lapse into their shared past, and he was all at once so tractable, so completely stripped of bluff. When she let him out into the drizzly night, she gave him a contemptuous pat for old times' sake. She could pity him, but she could not forget so easily his flareup when she broke her news. Curtis had behaved very badly. ...

... She couldn't sell him out! She couldn't run over him—why, God damn it! he would fix her, he had the goods on her, he would tell ... Suddenly two snake's eyes burned an inch from his. ... "You try to blackmail me, you double-crossing rat, and I'll cut your heart out!" ... He cringed. ... The exquisite Mrs. Potter resumed her seat, breathing ever so tremulously ... "You dirty little heel. ..."

Now it was over. And a good job, too, thought Mrs. Potter. It was always unpleasant dealing with Curtis, lately more than ever. He took too much for granted, got on a high horse and had to be knocked off. The nerve of him, claiming an interest in Whiteine! When her money, her brains, her labour put it over—and finally consummated a deliverance that would have paralyzed Curtis had he known the bargain she drove. She was going to be rich—rich. And he had the gall to try to stop her—to pull that formula stuff—to trot out a phony old recipe they had discarded in the first month of the business! Just the same, she had been wise to protect herself, to foresee the day when Curtis Rowlett's usefulness, and Whiteine's, would be ended and she could amputate both neatly, proceeding on her course with no mud from the old roads to clog that shining highway she discerned ahead.

Mrs. Potter went upstairs and made herself comfortable. She lay at ease among her pillows, staring at the opaque globe on the ceiling, and against its soft luminance the events, not of her past, but of her future shaped themselves. Today Neal Carver would have received her letter, tonight he might be reading it. Mrs. Potter sucked at the cigarette Cora Potts would never have approved. Its ribbons floated blue above her, and complacently she studied their loveliness. A slipper fell from her foot to the floor, "clump," and another. She let them lie.

Curtis was sunk. Whiteine was sunk. They were sunk with the past beyond resurrection. Sunk, she was confident, without a trace. Out—gone—unregretted—what the French called "feenee." And relief at their going went on their heels; relief was important only because of the freedom it gave for concentration on further affairs, of which Neal and Aseptiline were the chief, and the matter of America's three-billion-dollar Liberty Loan not to be ignored entirely.

The Liberty Loan campaign could wait for a couple of weeks; she was sure of herself there after the Red Cross triumph. It would be a social as well as a financial cinch. Aseptiline looked good. The New York advertising man had said you could sell anything to America if you had the capital to tell America about it often and long enough. Well, what it took to tell America she had. It was agreeable to own a business you weren't ashamed of. Next Sunday the Corinth newspapers were running announcements, with pictures of her and the factory, and the "American Magazine" was sending a woman all the way from New York to get the life story it had taken no little ingenuity to prepare. There remained Neal ...

She thought of him, not as a person, but as a utensil. He was another Mrs. Genelli, another fifty thousand Armenians, another bundle of "testimonial mail," or a German ship's crew. Formerly he had been, in some degree, a person, although even in that most personal of moments his significance to Mrs. Potter was clearly more utilitarian than human and individual. She had slaked hunger, as she had said, on the nearest dish. Then, while Neal was still admiring the novelty of his legs in puttees, his consequence as a person had evaporated utterly for her and his import as a utensil had towered. For certain happenings had suggested Neal for a master stroke.

They had begun as annoyances. A woman whom Mrs. Potter had met twice and chatted with at length, cut her dead on the street. Of course, the woman might have been nearsighted. But another woman, friend of the first, "postponed" a luncheon to which Mrs. Potter was invited. Later Mrs. Potter learned that the luncheon took place without a hitch; other guests, it seemed, had not been so regretfully forewarned. Then Bess Elton suddenly deserted Mrs. Potter's salon and Nancy Ann Morgan, flustered over the slip, explained what she meant when she said Mrs.

Potter's was "out of bounds for Bess." It appeared that Mrs. Elton was just a crazy old fussbox who despised everybody and by everybody was despised—nobody paid any attention to her, anyway! But the really serious blow fell with the story of the meeting at the Chamber of Commerce. The committee had chosen Mrs. Potter for the Liberty Loan job, but only after a Mr. Sims had bitterly protested and insisted that his vote be recorded against the disgrace of Corinth honouring a patent medicine quack— all matters which never saw print but were duly grapevined to Madam Chairman. It was that night Mrs. Potter informed the newspapers that she had an interesting story for them, after which she frankly sought Clark Burton's advice.

"I wouldn't worry," said that expert in social parcheesi, when she had confided all she deemed wise. "Primarily, my dear, it's this quaint enterprise of yours. You really can't expect the heirs of usurers and distillers to tolerate a cosmetic millionaire. Certainly not cosmetics for the Ethiopes! It is estimable to freeze them in tenements or peonize them in the cotton fields, but one mustn't get rich by offering them the same frauds white ladies delude themselves with. My, no!—it's not amusing, it's shocking, even a little dangerous. But you tell me you're reforming—profitably, I trust—and you'll find our memories graciously short. There's a deal of tainted money strutting around Corinth in boiled shirts and sables. No, I wouldn't worry over the tarbrush pursuing you. *Lamb fries* are delicacies by the time they reach the table, and your millions on the white folks' teeth won't be the same millions that bleached the black folks' faces. They'll be sanctified."

Mrs. Potter hadn't understood all his allusions, but she got the gist and the gist made sense. While Burton spouted around the room, she had listened serenely.

Suddenly he had stopped in front of her and waited, deliberately, until she raised her brows.

"The fact is, Genevieve, that isn't the whole truth. It isn't what people say about you that matters; it's why they say it. And they'll keep right on saying it—or something else—as long as you are what you are. Do you know what I mean? I can see you don't—you're glaring at me as though I had called you a strumpet. Look here—you're young, you're good-locking, you're rich, and you're living alone in Corinth. The first two are deadly enough, but with the last two added, you haven't a Chinaman's chance. Your money makes you a shining mark for gossip, and—you're living *alone* in *Corinth!* Do you understand! In New York, Paris, half a dozen cities, you'd take your fun and damn the torpedoes. But not in this town! I don't care how chaste you are—you can wear hair shirts and count your beads from now till doomsday—they'll crucify you sooner or later. And you're not chaste, my dear, are you?"

Then, in the same bland manner, he had asked her to marry him, and Mrs. Potter, bewildered and a little indignant, had declined. Certainly she was not going to wear a hair shirt to please anybody. Nor was she going to marry Clark Burton, either.

"No, thanks—I'm not marrying this week."

He had taken the refusal good-humouredly.

"Very well. ... I suppose I am only after your money. Still it wouldn't be a bad arrangement; I honestly believe I'd be worth the price. ... At least, the advice stands. I meant every word of it, lady—Corinth won't put up with Merry Widows off the stage. You ought to get married."

And so she would. She would marry blood and name and pride, and if poverty was there, too, it would not matter, for she had plenty for both, and blood would guard her, and name would challenge scandal, and pride would kill it if it dared. She would complete with Mendelssohn what Aseptiline had started. She would marry at once, and the man she would marry would not be a Clark Burton, whose cunning might be greater then her own, nor one of those stuffy patriots who bored her at luncheons, but a boy and a nice one, a boy like the chap who gave her his fraternity pin, like the boys who hung around Brundage's, like the young officers in their spurs and gold braid ... "Mrs. Genelli, do you know my husband, Captain Carver?"

Too bad in a way, thought Mrs. Potter, to have to do it like this, to have to put it up to him flat. But there was no more getting around it for her than there would be for him when he faced the inevitable—the thing was there like a sign-post, pointing the course that was not so much an opportunity as it was practically a duty to herself. The path had opened all at once. It had not been there, nor any seeming need of it, nor any thought of it, on the night she indulged a momentary urge. She had drowned thought that night; but apparently Providence had been thinking for her. And now, when new obstacles loomed, Providence opened the path chance had prepared. ... Already the affair was as good as concluded. He would come in, anxious, embarrassed, perhaps a little frightened and sullen, for he would have guessed what complication summoned him there. Yet it would not be necessary to plead or argue or shed a tear—she knew her man of honour too well—only to state the expected and let her head droop once. If, and she thought it scarcely likely, he was for desperate means, she had her answer, and he would be too inexperienced to know better. ... So Providence would conquer. So the utensil would fit the hand, and the path open to receive her. She would be Mrs. Carver, Mrs. Captain Neal Carver, and the world could hush its mouth. ...

Would Neal look nice in uniform? For a moment she thought of him as a person, and she was glad that he was young and handsome. It was almost too bad there was not, and never was, about to be a little Neal. ...

CHAPTER FIFTEEN
OMNIA VINCIT VISCERA

A T ELEVEN O'CLOCK the rector of All Souls Church stopped his Ford sedan at the end of the row of poplars, locked it against tempted sinners, and bounded across the lawn to his study. It was a bright, golden morning, with the first haze of Indian Summer creeping along the distant hedgerows. The rector of All Souls was full of breakfast well digested, he had a pleasant duty before him, and he was in ample time to prepare for it.

In his study he lit a cigar, unbuttoned the bottom button of his vest, settled himself comfortably, and opened the Prayer Book to page 220. He knew as well as he knew the Beatitudes the form for the solemnization of matrimony, but there was always the possibility of the most familiar line eluding one and he disliked to consult the book during the ceremony.

He read rapidly.

"Dearly beloved, we are gathered here together in the sight of God, and in the face of this company, to join together this Man and this Woman in holy Matrimony ... an honourable estate ... not to be entered into unadvisably or lightly. ... If any man can show just cause why they may not lawfully be joined together, let him now speak. ... For be ye well assured that if any persons are joined together otherwise than as God's Word doth allow, their marriage is not lawful. ...

"Wilt thou have this Woman—"

The rector of All Souls laid down the Prayer Book, he hunted in his pocket until he found the memorandum he sought, he picked up the Prayer Book and made light notations on the side of the page. The spot was worn with many light notations and erasures. ... "Neal" ... "Genevieve" ... Pleasant names. The rector smiled appreciatively. The last ones had been George and Mehitabel, and he still remembered their wedding with mortification.

"Neal, wilt thou have this woman—"

Outside the study door, through the chancel, the notes of an organ began to throb. Mr. Medthorne, the organist, practised softly but painstakingly. There was a quaver almost of anxiety in his tremolo. "Tristan" had been his own choice, not the bride's, and he was apprehensive. These rich women always were powers in the church, and though this one had sent word that she didn't care, you never could tell—she might prefer "O, Promise Me," and Mr. Medthorne was a poor man who depended on his salary.

While Mr. Medthorne played, a florist's assistant puttered around the altar, putting the final touches to the banked flowers. Sunshine filtered in long streamers through the lofty windows, staining the flowers with the gold and crimson and purple of the dying Christ. They were Marechal Niel roses, but they seemed like enormous bunches of vari-coloured sweet peas.

The sexton joined the florist's assistant, and the two stood looking at the flowers and discussing the wedding.

The florist's assistant was of the opinion that the people must not be much, since they had ordered so few flowers for a church wedding. But the sexton explained that it was one of those hurry-up affairs. The man was in the Army and no telling when he would have to go to war. He reckoned the girl had insisted on getting married in church. Women were like that. They'd notified *him* only the night before—and lucky they were to get the church with all these war weddings going on.

"Brass buttons gets 'em," said the florist's assistant. "What I say is, 'Marry in haste and repent in leisure.' There's gonna be a many a pair bust up after this war's over."

At eleven-thirty Clark Burton appeared. Resplendent in morning clothes, he stood in the shadowy aisle, explaining to the sexton about the seating. The florist's assistant, eyeing Mr. Burton, was more impressed.

There would be no ushers, none of the usual attendants. The sexton understood that the wedding was very sudden. But everything must be correct—the bride had entrusted all details to Mr. Burton. The groom's family would sit over there. Only three of them, but probably the groom would sit there, too, until the actual ceremony. No marching in or anything of that sort, only music. The bride would sit on the other side with Burton. Nobody else unless she arrived with friends. As for the others, it didn't matter—anywhere back there would do. Probably there wouldn't be much of a crowd—

An outburst of little shrieks drew Mr. Burton toward the vestibule, the sexton following him up the aisle with his expectations of a large tip suddenly revived by Mr. Burton's pants and Mr. Burton's boutonnière and Mr. Burton's general air of elegance.

Four young ladies filled the vestibule with exclamation. From their rapture and excitement, the sexton judged they had not seen one another in years, but after listening while they surrounded Mr. Burton, he gathered that the furore was all on account of the wedding, which was thrilling, cute, grand, marvellous and amazing, though two at least of the young ladies, it developed, had been sure of it all the time because of the way somebody always looked at somebody else.

The sexton jogged Mr. Burton's elbow.

"Here come some more," he said.

An automobile had stopped in front of the church, depositing a large lady who tinkled like a cluster of prisms as she hurried up the walk.

"My dear, I had such a time!—and I only heard last night—dear Mrs. Potter!—I telephoned her—"

Soon another car drew up, and a third and a fourth, and from these issued more ladies, and a few gentlemen, some of them old and some of them young. The sexton recognized prominent parishioners—Mrs. Stanley Sartain, old Mrs. Wentworth, members of the Tennyson family. ... Well, this was to be a classy wedding, hurry-up or not!

The church was spottily but rapidly filling. The sexton had no more ushered in one group than he must hotfoot back for another, and Mr. Burton was busy as a floorwalker, shaking hands, smiling, saying, "Yes—yes—we were all surprised—she'll be glad you came just the same—so will the Carvers—oh, they knew all along!—But Neal wanted it this way—has to report back to camp tomorrow, you know—none but the brave—"

In the midst of one of these conversations Mr. Burton stopped and gripped the sexton's arm.

"The family—"

Four persons were coming up the walk—a natty looking old gentleman with a pretty girl on his arm, and behind them a pale, frail lady whose companion was a young man in khaki.

"Looks scared," thought the sexton—"the lucky stiff!"

For by this time the sexton had learned that the betrothed of the young man was worth not less than two million dollars.

Meanwhile, at about the moment that the rector of All Souls was loosening the bottom button of his vest, Mrs. Genevieve Potter hurried alone down the stone steps of the Cheney place and sharply ordered Josef to drive to the Nickajack Building. She was dressed in tan silk, with a hat of darker shade, and she carried a small bouquet of orchids and lilies of the valley. She looked charming—all but her eyes. These were hot holes.

Behind her, in the house where wrappings and garments cluttered the rooms, she left a maid in tears and a butler who could not move two steps from the telephone without its peal recalling him. For hours, since Corinth woke to the brief announcement in the morning paper, he had been repeating the same singsong. Very sorry—Mrs. Potter was busy. Yes, the report was true. At eleven o'clock, All Souls Church ... Mrs. Corwin? He would give Mrs. Potter the message and he was instructed to say, in case any of Mrs. Potter's friends called, that there had been no time to issue invitations and she would be very happy if they cared to attend the wedding. ...

One call Mrs. Potter had taken herself. The man had been insistent; unless the butler was mightily mistaken, it was that po' white trash, Mr. Rowlett. He had told the butler he would come out there and whale the black skin off him if he didn't get his mistress to the 'phone. The butler had obeyed, but afterward he was sorry, for it was then Mrs. Potter had busted the vase, and laid into him and the maid, and Lordy knows!—she had been in a big enough scrabble before that. ...

A bride in a rage. ...

Josef drove fast, for there was not much time, less than an hour from the Cheney place to town and then back to the church. Yet time enough for what she purposed, which was the burning up of Curtis Rowlett. ... No man could threaten her! Let alone a little skunk who tried it on her wedding day. ... "You'll be sorry if you don't ... sorry if you don't... She would, huh? God help his soul! ... The car streaked through the bright morning, but if any waved, or any stopped and bowed, they got no recognition from the pretty lady with the orchids and valley lilies. She stared straight ahead, and Corinth intruded on the focus of those two hot holes no more than the sunshine and the blue and dimpled sky.

In the plaza before the Nickajack Building something was going on around the municipal flagpole. A crowd thickened, workmen tacked the last pieces of bunting to a small stand, and Mrs. Potter saw the flash of band instruments and a man in a frock coat.

She recalled that this was the day of Corinth's hail and farewell to the first soldiers of the new National Army, the conscripts of the draft. She had even promised to be there, with the Mayor and the Public Safety Committee and other civic leaders, on the platform when the lads from desk and counter straggled by.

No matter now. The car had to make a detour, Josef's horn bleating, and Mrs. Potter jiggled her knees impatiently as the crowd divided before the slowly moving wheels.

"Wait here, Josef. If a cop kicks, tell him who you are. Tell him I'm on the Mayor's committee."

It was a quick ascent to the eleventh floor. When she got off the elevator, she did not enter the main offices of Complexion Refineries, but traversed the corridor until she reached an unmarked door. A girl, passing, looked hard at the flowers, and at the woman without recognition; Complexion Refineries had not seen Mrs. Potter in months and new help was numerous in that time.

Mrs. Potter knocked. Curtis opened almost at once.

She closed the door and, standing just inside it, said nothing until he had crossed the room and right-about-faced, leaning against his desk with one ankle swung over the other and hands in his pockets. Curtis was a little man—he had never weighed more than a hundred and thirty—and now, with even the sallow mud drained out of his face, he looked puny and dirty and sick, like some unhealthy fungus dragged out of a cellar and propped up in sham truculence. She thought she had never realized how skinny he was.

Well, no use wasting words on this shrimp.

"Get this, Curtis. I'm here only because you don't seem to understand one thing. I'm through with you. As definitely through as though you were dead. If you ever dare speak to me—"

Curtis ripped one hand out, clawing it up and down in the air.

"Shut up! ... You did the talking last time. I'm talking now. I didn't get you down here to blah-blah at me. I'm telling you! I'm telling what you're going to do! Will you listen to me? Will you listen to me?"

He still leaned on the desk, but his hand jerked, up and down, up and down, as though he would bat her quiet, and she was astonished at his vehemence.

"Well—say it! I'm in a hurry."

"I know." He pulled himself together, smirking maliciously. "You're going to marry that willy-boy, aren't you? Well, you're not. ... You're not unless you get me out of the jam I'm in and do it damn quick."

"What jam?"

He swallowed. His rat's eyes scuttled and blinked. He was obviously in a sweat of fear, physically unable *to* speak. Then—

"Jail," said Curtis, "for embezzlement."

The words dropped into a puddle of silence, so still that the murmur of the crowd in the plaza came up through the open window with separate voices distinguishable. A man shouted, "Tom! Tom Bell!" And while the ripples widened in Mrs. Potter's brain, she wondered if she knew anyone named Tom Bell and thought that it was nearly time for the parade to start and that she must get away before traffic was held up.

"What do you mean, Curtis?"

"Shucks—you know what I mean. What's the use of stalling? I stole money—the firm's money—your money, if you like! ... I been grabbing my little cut for a long time. Oh, not much! Don't get scared—I didn't have the guts to swipe much, worse luck. You never would have found out—it wouldn't be found out now if you hadn't of shot the business out from under me!" His voice suddenly rose shrill. "But you sicked those damn auditors onto me before I had a chance to make good! They're out there now, they got the books, and I'm scared, Thelma, I'm scared! For Christ's sake, Thelma, don't let 'em send me to jail!"

He was twitching, both hands out, opening and shutting in a kind of clumsy appeal, yet he still leaned on the desk with his ankles crossed, only his hands weaving and his head butted forward as though he were tied and would pull himself to her by his haggard eyes.

Thelma only glared at him above her flowers.

"All right. ..."

Curtis dropped his arms, twisted about and snatched something from his desk. He waved it, a small black book. She had seen it before—where?

"You won't, huh? Then look here. Know what this is? ... You wouldn't! ... Thought I was pretty dumb, huh? Thought I was a sucker you could string along and kick in the pants when you got ready? Well, you can't get away with that stuff, Mrs. Cora Potts Thelma LaMont Potter! That's what's in that book—the whole dirty, rotten, stinking story! With names and dates and facts, enough dynamite to blow you to hell and back! ... You and your society friends and your God-damned nance you think you're going to marry! ... Marry! Do you think he'd marry you once he gets a look at this? Do you think he'll love his sweet little Genevieve when he knows she let a guy keep her when she was fifteen, and practically murdered him, and ran the most notorious chippy house in Peachburg for ten years—"

He strangled in his own filth, coughing and shaking, but brandishing the book like a tomahawk.

"Yes!" … He spat. … "Yes, you'll marry him! … All right, you will. But first you're going to come clean with me. You're going to get me out of this jam, you understand? You're going to fix those auditors or else call off the deal—I don't give a damn how you work it—but you'll keep me out of jail and keep my job to boot. This is a showdown, you understand? There's going to be another contract right now. … Or if there ain't, I damn well leave this office in the next five minutes. And you know where I'm going."

Ghastly in his fear and hope, he waited. He had shot his bolt.

Mrs. Potter did not stir for several minutes. Both hands clutched the flowers. She held them at her breast so that their faint scent rose in her nostrils. She stood very straight. Presently, across her staring gaze, a sort of blanket seemed to fall. She placed her right foot forward.

Curtis drew back; he whisked the book behind him. But Mrs. Potter did not swerve an inch, she passed him without a glance, and as she reached the window and looked out, holding the flowers lightly now, there was about her nothing different from the manner of any lady who had crossed a room to admire the view.

There was nothing to tell him, watching, desperate, teeth set, whether it was peace or war. There was nothing in the trim shoulders, nothing in the cock of the smart hat, to show what went on in that head, whether she saw, between her and the midgets far below, red haze or pale defeat, or a lifetime of constant panic and repeated surrender. …

Sudden music, a roar of cheers, burst from the street.

"Look, Curtis!" cried Mrs. Potter. "Look—it's the drafted boys! By golly—it's niggers!"

"Aw, nuts!" snarled Curtis.

"No, really—you ought to see them."

Her head turned; she was laughing.

Clutching the book under one arm, he went to the window. Some way off, as he leaned out, he could see flags and an irregular column, black faces glistening in the sunshine. Mrs. Potter stepped quickly back. ...

A wind seemed to puff the book from under his arm, he straightened only to feel a stunning blow at the base of his spine, and as he clawed at nothing, the plaza was a bright juggernaut rushing up at him enormously. ...

In the centre of the room, Mrs. Potter dusted the tips of her gloves. For a second she studied the open window. ... He had been very puny. ... Then, picking up the book and the bouquet, she made her exit without haste or delay, closing the door behind her. She glanced at her wrist watch. It was a quarter to twelve.

Josef, standing in the front seat of the car, pointed excitedly toward the struggling throng on the corner. People ran past as she left the building.

"A man, madam—fell or jumped, I don't know which."

"How awful! ... Hurry, Josef! I can't be late for my own wedding."

She could have told him, she reflected. She could have explained that it was one more embezzler, taking the only way out. ... But she didn't.

Sunshine glittered after the Potter car. Policemen sped it on its way. From block to block, bits of paper fluttered behind it. At last, a gloved hand emerged, tossing a black scrap into the gutter.

Clark Burton ceased fidgeting on the steps of All Souls Church, sighed with relief, gently fingered his cravat and extended his bent right arm.

The bride went in. Music embraced her. Lilies touched her lips.

THE END

www.ingramcontent.com/pod-product-compliance
Lightning Source LLC
Chambersburg PA
CBHW030126260626
47156CB00008B/2809